"I gotta pee."

That was my first thought. It's not a deep thought, but there is something inherently profound about declaring the truth, even if it is a simple truth based on need and instinct. So it's not a deep thought. It's not even an unusual thought. I would guess throughout the world men share a similar thought every morning as the rooster crows. The thought might come in different cultures and different languages, but the meaning is still basically the same. "I need to relieve myself of this pressing desire."

I don't know if women have the same thought. I wouldn't dare assume anything about women. For one thing, my experience with women has been fairly limited. I am only twenty years old, after all. Well, I guess I'm actually sixty years old, but I'll explain that in a little bit. The other thing is, men who have had a lot more experience with women tell me they still don't understand them. Besides, this kind of thing doesn't come up in polite conversation. And there is another difference between men and women. Men don't mind having impolite conversations.

I kind of like the thought that most, if not all, men have the same basic thought in the morning. It's an equalizer of sorts. It doesn't matter if you are a prince or a peon. You could be a monarch or a mechanic. The fact is we all need to relieve ourselves.

So the only thing a little unusual about my particular thought is I have a catheter in me and so I shouldn't be feeling the pressure build up. And, I suppose, the fact I've had a catheter in my body for about forty years, give or take a day or two.

Nope, scratch that thought. According to the chronometer right above and to the left of my face, it has been in me for exactly forty years, now only plus or minus a few hours. I guess maybe I need to explain a few things. For that to happen, I should start at the beginning.

My name is Blue. I know, it's an unusual name, and it ain't much of a name at all, but it's the only name I got. Honestly. I don't have a last name. To have one of those you need to have a mom and dad, and I didn't have either of those either. Okay, I had someone who said things like, "Of course I love you, darling" and "Sure, I'll still respect you in the morning." And I had some scared teenager who thought her particular idiot would keep his promises. She probably hid the pregnancy from her parents until I popped out before getting kicked to the curb for being a whore. I'm guessing about everything so far because during that time I was still an egg sitting inside a nice warm nest and had no idea what was going on in the world around me, kind of like I am right now.

My mom, whoever she was, decided to find me a better home by putting me in the back of a pickup truck parked at the feed store. Why a feed store? Beats me. I guess she was thinking farmers parked at feed stores and they might need another hand someday. Or maybe she was thinking someone who cared for animals would know how to care for a baby. Wasn't much difference, right? Either way, I ended up in the bed of a Ford pick-up belonging to Mr. Ezekiel Jones, a colored man farming a homestead of forty acres with his bride of thirty years, Mrs. Martha Jones.

Now I have to bring race into the story. I don't want to, but people in those days cared about such things and I suppose people still do. Time doesn't change some things in people.

You see, I was about as white as white could be and this was the south. We could have been at the North Pole and it still would have been a problem for a black couple to raise a foundling white baby at that time. But Zeke, as he liked to be called, didn't see things in black and white, so to speak. He said all men were colored, but God chose different crayons to color each of them. I wish more people felt like Zeke. Maybe they do now, but I kind of doubt it.

Things worked out well for a time. Zeke and Martha raised me like their own flesh and blood. They had lost their own son in the jungles of Vietnam. The government said he had been there as an "advisor", whatever that means. All his parents knew was their son left a hole in the jungles of Vietnam to come home to a hole in the ground.

Things were working out pretty good. Zeke

named me Blue because when he found me I was in a blue jumper with a trumpet on it. He said I was his little boy blue, blowing on his horn.

Martha wanted to call me Gideon, who blew a trumpet in the Old Testament. Or maybe Gabriel who blows the trump of God. But, in the end, Zeke got his way and I was called Blue. Gideon or Gabriel might have been better for me. After all, there isn't much call to pick on someone named after a Bible character, but Blue is a name begging to be picked on.

Like I said, things were working out pretty good for all of us. I learned to read by the time I was four, mostly out of the Bible. I could add and subtract small numbers and could count to at least a hundred. I also knew how to do some farm chores and was expected to have them done before breakfast. I was happy. They were happy.

Until I insisted on going with Zeke to get farm supplies. Some good "Christian" folks decided a white child didn't belong with a black couple, not in mid sixties Arkansas anyways. Such things might have been all right for them "Yankees" up North, but down here they knew better.

This is where my view of God gets a little fuzzy for the first time. It's not the first time he gets a little out of focus in my vision. In fact, he's a bit little fuzzy in my vision at the moment.

Zeke and Martha were good Christians. They

went church every Sunday. It was all day Sunday. They would sing and dance in praises to God before the preacher started his sermon, which would get interrupted by more singing and dancing with praises to God. But he didn't mind. In fact, there were times he would interrupt himself to start singing out praises.

Supposedly, the good folk who saw me with Zeke and realized he had custody of me felt it was their "Christian" duty to yank me out of a perfectly good home and stick me in the foster care system. Being six at the time meant I was too old to realistically look forward to being adopted; besides, I didn't want anyone but Zeke and Martha to adopt me. They were my parents!

So, instead, I got shuffled from one foster home to another. Looking back with fourteen years of life's experience under my belt, I try not to blame the good folks who yanked me away from my family. Honestly, I try. Okay, maybe I didn't try all that much in the beginning, but I realized later they were doing what was expected of them at the time.

Of course, living in the moment, I blamed anyone and everyone I could, so I ended up in many different foster homes and spent more than a few months in either juvenile court or as part of a group home. The only reason I was taken out from time to time and placed with a family is because I was lean, healthy, and well muscled. This meant, of course, I was a source of cheap labor. Why hire a farm hand to work in your fields when it was easier to grab a kid out of the foster system for awhile and sending him back when the majority of the work was done.

Come to think of it, cheap labor wasn't the only reason I was placed with families. One fine Christian gentleman decided to use me as a play thing when I was around thirteen. He was a Deacon or some such garbage at one of the larger churches in his hometown. He also taught a youth class and would often take a large group of boys out for camping trips, where he would teach some of them something not found in any decent book, much less the "good book".

When he came for me, I had the knife Zeke had given me for my sixth birthday, several fine lessons from some of my fellow fosters, and about seven years of pent up rage and frustration building up inside of me. I went back to the foster system the next day and he went away with a warning I knew where he lived and would come visit sometime when he least expected me. I heard he moved a short time later. I also heard about his death a year or so later. I wasn't surprised or disappointed.

Another lady wanted me for about the same purposes. A firm no and the threat to tell her husband convinced her she didn't want me nearly as bad as she had thought at first.

Despite all of the problems, I managed to make it to my eighteenth birthday and barely managed to stay in school long enough to get my High School diploma. I wasn't exactly an honor grad, but I made a few A's and B's with mostly C's. I wasn't heading to college on those grades, but they were good enough for the Army.

I have to admit, the only reason I made it as far as I did was due to the influence of my parents. Yes, I still call them that, though I rarely got to see them after the system took me away. Rarely may not be the right word, but it wasn't often enough to suit either me or them. They sent me money on my birthday and bought me presents at Christmas. They managed to teach me a thing or two along the way as well. It was their calming influence and sure faith God was going to work all things together for good that kept me straight enough to stay out of jail so I could join the Army.

They even came to my Basic training graduation up in Fort Leonard Wood, Missouri. I was so proud to see them I thought sure I was going to pop a button off of my chest.

That's the other time my view of God clouded somewhat. Despite all of the good they had done, not only in helping to raise me, but for other people as well, the two people I had loved most in the world were killed by a drunk driver on their way home from my graduation. I blamed myself. I blamed the drunk driver. I blamed the bartender who served him. I blamed the whole world. But most of all, I blamed God. He was in control after all.

I could have gone completely off the rails at that point. I probably would have, but Zeke and Martha were still with me in a way. Every lesson they taught me echoed in my mind. Besides, I didn't want to shame their memories. So instead, I threw myself into anything and everything the Army sent my way. I was going into Military Intelligence as an analyst. It wasn't the exciting spy stuff I thought it would be, but it kept my mind busy and I was good at it. I think part of the reason I was so good at it was because of my upbringing. You wouldn't think getting jerked from home to home would help anyone in any way, but it taught me a few things.

For one thing, I had learned about adapting myself into whatever culture I found myself in. I know, it wasn't like I was traveling to far off lands, but each of my foster homes had a unique way of looking at things and a unique way of wanting things done. The best way to stay out of trouble and away from the paddle or whatever form of punishment they wanted to use, was to adapt to their way of thinking as quickly as I could.

I also learned to read people quickly in their culture. Each family has their own set of rules they play by and every person in a family reacts to their circumstances according to those rules. So I could anticipate those reactions if I could read them quick enough. It wasn't much of an edge, but it kept me out of trouble more than once.

I now turned those skills to reading intelligence reports we received. Most people had a hard time getting out of their own cultural background. I didn't have one to get out of. I guess maybe I had several to choose from and still adapted to them as the circumstances called for.

It was my rare ability that helped get me chosen for a new project NASA was working on. Well, that and the fact I didn't have anyone anywhere who was going to miss me if were to disappear for around forty years.

NASA was planning on sending men into deep space, but even at the speed of light, which we couldn't even get close to at the time, meant that any astronaut going out there was going to be long dead before he reached his destination. So the only choice was to put several couples on a spaceship, hope they had a couple of kids each, and then hope that those kids got along well enough to have kids of their own, so that in the end, the grandkids of the original astronauts would plant Old Glory on some foreign planet. It wasn't very practical, so they came up with suspended animation.

I was the guinea pig. Actually, I think I was one of several test subjects. Some of them went to sleep for only a year or so, while others, like myself, got extended stays in dreamland.

That's where my ability to adapt supposedly came in handy. Since no one knew what the culture would be like in forty years, they thought it would be a good idea to send a cultural chameleon on ahead.

I know what you are thinking. What good would it do to have someone sleep for forty years? Well the good people at NASA didn't have the propulsion worked out. In fact, there were a whole lot of things worked out. They were hoping that by the time they had all of the other details worked out, like propulsion and so on, that they would also know that their suspended animation system worked because they would send Princess Charming to come kiss me and wake me up. Boy, talk about morning breath! I wouldn't want to kiss anyone until I had a gallon of mouthwash and a power scrubber for my teeth.

My problem at the moment, though, is that I gotta pee. I know I keep coming back to that and it probably sounds like no big deal, but, trust me, it is. If I gotta pee, and I do, then the systems are all shutting down and it's time for me to come out of my cocoon as a golden butterfly. The only problem is that I can't open the door from the inside. Even if there were latches on the inside for me to open, my arms are still pinned down and I can't move them at all. This was meant to simulate space travel, so the wise folks decided that their passengers for the great beyond should be strapped in tight so that they didn't float around in their cocoon and get jostled about by the movement of the spacecraft.

It all made perfect sense, except the part where

the astronaut dies either from lack of oxygen, starvation, dehydration, or an exploded bladder, the last of which I was sure to die from.

I'm not the sharpest knife in the drawer, but I think I would have figured out some kind of failsafe for opening the door from the inside. Again, I wasn't the only one put to sleep, so to speak. One or more of the others had automated systems on their capsules. They were the mission commanders who were supposed to wake up first and then wake everyone else up. So either they developed amnesia, a case of I don't give a crap, or their capsule never opened or they were asleep forever.

I was about to give up on rescue and hopefully drift back into deep sleep, making for a more peaceful transition when I finally went from temporary sleep to the permanent kind. I know, it sounds like I'm a quitter, and maybe so, but I knew that no amount of pounding, kicking, or screaming was going to help. For one thing, my straps kept me from doing either of the first two, and I knew the capsule was soundproof. My only hope was to drift back into sleep and hopefully never wake up.

I know that sounds like a desperation ploy, but it was my only hope. I needed to relax as much as possible. I needed to slow down my breathing, drop my heart rate and use as little as oxygen as possible in the hope that whoever was supposed to open my capsule would get there soon. In the meantime, all I could do was wait.

Wait a minute. Maybe I was panicking for nothing. Maybe I wasn't really awake after all. Shortly after I entered the capsule, I had a dream, a nightmare really, about this very thing. I dreamt that a massive earthquake had caused a landslide that covered my location. After some time, don't ask me how long since time has no real meaning for me, my brain realized that it was only a nightmare and allowed me to relax again. So maybe I was dreaming now. It was possible, I suppose.

Most people, including the scientists who put me in here, assumed that there wouldn't be any brain activity during suspended animation, but the mind is a funny thing and it decides, for the most part, when, where, and how it will or will not function. I dreamed, had thoughts, passed the time making up crosswords in my head, and listened to the various stories and music that was piped in thru small speakers on either side of my head.

One of the scientists thought that some brain activity was possible and that it might also be possible for the mind to atrophy, the way muscles do. To combat muscle atrophy, they hooked me up to electrodes that provided mild electrical impulses that caused my muscles to contract. I wasn't going to look like a superhero when the door opened, but maybe I could hold my head up and walk with only a little help.

The mind, on the other hand, doesn't respond well to having electrodes placed on it and receiving mild electrical shocks. So they came up with a different plan. They had books stored on a computer and had them play over and over on a loop. There was everything from the classics like Moby Dick and The Three Musketeers to science fiction by Asimov and Heinlein to language learning tapes in Spanish, French, and German. Knowing my luck, I would come out speaking some strange combination of those three and English. I made sure they included a copy of the Bible. They wanted me to have the Koran and some other sacred texts to, but I refused. I wasn't exactly on speaking terms with God when I entered the capsule and didn't feel like being introduced to other gods who would end up being just as, if not more, disappointing.

One of the sociologists made sure they included several romance novels. It wasn't my idea of a good time, but she my track record with women was less than stellar from our interviews and thought the romance novels might help me gain a little insight.

Suddenly there was a face in the glass above me. She was the most beautiful woman I had ever seen. The words stunning and exquisite came to mind. I'll admit I didn't have much to compare her to in my short twenty years before going into deep sleep, but she was absolutely breathtaking.

So I said the first thing that came to my mind, "I

gotta pee."

So much for romance novels.

CHAPTER TWO

Then I knew I had been dreaming again because the face disappeared. It was obvious that a face that beautiful could only exist in the imagination. Then I realized that the nightmare was back. The porthole glass went totally black. I had been covered up by tons of dirt and debris and would never be found again. Until, that is, archaeologists made a startling discovery hundreds or even thousands of years from now and dug up my well preserved but very dead body. Oh well, at least I'd be good for something.

The blackness disappeared and small lights came into focus. As I studied the lights, I realized that they were forming letters and that those letters were in turn forming words. It took me a little time to make out what they were saying. I wasn't an idiot, but this was the first time I had seen anything in print for forty years. Slowly, very slowly, the thoughts and ideas of words returned back to me.

"I'm here to open the capsule. Are you alright?"

The blackness left and the beautiful face reappeared. I had never been so glad to see a face in all my life. She could have looked like the wicked witch combined with Quasimodo and I still would have been glad to see her, but the fact that she looked like an angel sure did help. I tried to answer her, but my lips wouldn't move. I couldn't even nod my head. My face must have reflected my panic, because the face left and the blackness reappeared, along with more words in lights.

"It's okay. We expected this. Just blink if you are alright."

My rescuing angel came back into view once more. I blinked once, then about a thousand times as the moisture suddenly returned to my dry eyes. I must have looked like an idiot, but she seemed amused. She smiled brightly and then left again. More words.

"Close your eyes. I need to spray you with disinfectant."

That I understood. The people who put me in here told me I'd probably be carrying diseases that had been wiped out by the time I was recovered. I would be a walking Petri dish to my new home. It would be like transporting someone from the past into our time. That's something they don't talk much about on the sci-fi flicks. So I obediently closed my eyes while she fiddled with knobs, pulled switches and turned whatever else she needed to do to get me out of here. I waited patiently; my bladder was in a hurry, though.

With a hiss and a rush of cool air, I was almost free. It was then that I realized that the good people who put me in here had insisted I not wear any clothes. I wasn't exactly ashamed of my physique, at least as it had been forty years ago. I'm sure the electrodes that stimulated my muscles were doing an adequate job, but I wasn't exactly ready to display everything I had to first woman I met, especially when she was as absolutely gorgeous as this one. I was about to say something when I felt to first spray of mist start spraying at my feet. It quickly worked its way up along my legs and was soon at my loins. So much for modesty.

I comforted myself with that thought that my rescuer was probably a scientist, or maybe a doctor. At the very least she was a nurse or some other kind of caregiver. She had probably seen a host of men during her practice and the sight of my naked body meant no more to her than an ingrown toenail to a podiatrist.

"My name is Jackee," she sang. I know, she didn't literally sing, but her voice was so melodic and sweet that it sounded like a song. I think she could probably read names out of the phone book and it would sound like a choir of angels.

"I'll be your nurse and primary caregiver for the next forty-eight hours or so, allowing you time to assimilate into society," she continued in that lovely voice. "I'm sure you have many questions and we have quite a few for you as well, as you can imagine." I would have told her my life story from beginning to end if she wanted to hear it. And if that wasn't enough, I would tell her the life story of anyone she wanted to hear about. I would do or say just about anything for her. I know, I was falling in love way too quick.

Miss Martha used to say, "I think you spell that kind of love, L U S T." I could hear her voice echoing through the halls of my memory and I'm pretty sure she was right, but could anyone really blame me? She was absolutely gorgeous and I hadn't seen a woman outside of my dreams for forty years. A guy can't help being a guy sometimes.

"Keep your eyes closed a little longer, please," she asked. Till doomsday if she wanted. "I'm going to start removing the leads for your muscle contractions, along with the IV lines, and the...."

"No," I screamed in my mind. I knew what she was about to say and it couldn't happen. I would jerk it out myself before I'd let her do it. I would, but my arms and legs were still pinned, and even if they weren't, I don't think I could move at this point. There was nothing more degrading, demoralizing, more emasculating than what she was about to say.

".....catheter," she finished. She finished and so was I. I couldn't possibly hope to have any chance to ask her out now. I was just a patient and always would be from this point on. A sad, shrunken, pathetic little patient.

"For a sixty year old specimen," she said. Was it just me or had her voice lost its melodic tone? Had it taken on a more clinical tone? I'm sure it had. I think I stopped listening. "You have a very fine physique." Did she say what I think she did? Maybe there was still a little bit of a song in her voice after all.

"Almost through," she sang. "The mist that was sprayed on you also has an anesthetic effect. We realized the various probes and wires had been on you, or in you for some time." Even as she said that last part, I felt the catheter pull loose. There was no pain, just a slight release of pressure.

Pressure!?! Oh please, no. On top of everything else, don't let me do that. Not here. Not now. Not with her still standing there looking at me. I had held it for forty years, hadn't I? No, not in reality. The catheter had been allowing me release for the last forty years and now it was gone and I had already been feeling pressure building against the dam. If the dam was now gone, what was going to stop me from releasing a flood? I'm glad she still wanted me to keep my eyes closed. Of course, the cool mist that was still spraying over my body wasn't helping matters any. For some reason, "Singing in the Rain" started playing in my head. Only I didn't have a glorious feeling. I had a feeling I was about to crawl back into my little cocoon and go to sleep for another forty years, but I also had the feeling that when I woke up they would still be talking about it.

"Remember what he did to poor Jackee?" One would say.

"Get the umbrellas handy and make sure to wear your rain gear," another would answer.

"Don't worry," Jackee's voice now. "I understand what you must be going through. But you won't be able to stand for another couple of minutes, so you better let me help a little. Don't be embarrassed. It's something all of us have to do." I couldn't argue with here. Really, I couldn't because the mist was still coming up my chest and I couldn't open my mouth. But that didn't stop other things from opening up. I felt something come up around the dam area and felt her give a slight pressure to help things start. And that's all it took was a slight pressure. At least I didn't give her a shower. I could be thankful for that much. I guess she could be thankful too, since I think it would have been a long shower.

"Better," she asked/stated. It wasn't really, but what could I do? I sensed her back away as the mist came back down again. I was beginning to feel like my old car on a Saturday afternoon before a big date. It was the only time it got a thorough cleansing and I hate to say it, but it didn't get clean as often as I would have liked. I felt her begin toweling me dry. I guess the next step would be a hot wax and buffing to a high polish. She had already checked the fluids and I was probably now at least a quart low. Oh, and did I mention the backfire? Yeah, that's something else that had built up over the years. The towel was wiping off my chest now. Was she taking her time there? She seemed to be rubbing over the same areas like laps on a track.

"Wow," she almost gushed. "I don't think I've ever seen a chest with so much hair. Come to think of it, I don't think I've ever seen a hairy chest. I like it." And to prove she did like it, she continued to rub the towel over that area for quite some time. I suppose that since she was drying me off, the mist was over and I could open my eyes, but they didn't seem to want to open just yet, and who could blame them? After all, there was still the theory out there that I was still fast asleep in my cocoon and this was just another in a (short) list of fantasies my mind concocted while I was asleep.

"I really like it," she reassured. And I think she giggled. Or did she growl? I'm not sure and I'm not sure it matters. I was off the patient list. I felt her start to loosen the straps that held down my extremities, beginning with my legs. Feeling was coming back a little at a time and I almost think I could wiggle my toes. My fingers contracted, curled, and stretched, flexing my forearm muscles as they did.

"Nice." I was pleased she liked it. Maybe in a few minutes I could flex my biceps and really impress her. Then after a week or so, we could walk along the beach and I could kick sand into some wimps face. I could feel the blood pulsing through arteries, veins, and capillaries. Feeling was coming back to every part of my body. Part of it wasn't too comfortable and wanted to reject that feeling of prickly pain, but I had come too far to give in now.

"Alright," Jackee said, "I think it's time for you to open your eyes and come back to the land of the living. Let me help you sit up." I opened my eyes and eased my torso forward and that's when all the feeling left my body again.

Somebody once said something about the more things change, the more they stay the same. Whoever said that was an idiot.

Fashion changes. I remember watching Hee Haw with one of my foster families. I don't think I would have picked the show on my own. I was more into rock or maybe the blues. But I remember that show because the collars were so big and so long that they could have been used as wings in a high wind. I'm surprised we never read about someone losing an eye as the result of their collar sticking up.

Everything changes and nothing more so than fashion in my lifetime. I know, because I've seen my fair share of it in the short twenty years I had on earth before I took a long Siesta. I remember the stuffed suits of the sixties with their starched shirts, wide ties, and highly polished shoes giving way to fringed leather vests, tie-dyed t-shirts, and sandals. Then there were bell-bottomed pants and platform shoes. What a combination that was.

And of course, no one can forget, even if we really wanted to, double knit polyester pants. I had a pair of lime green ones that I purposely wore to welding class so some sparks could "accidentally" fall on them. My legs got burned and so did my backside, but I would take several more whippings just to get rid of those pants. Whoever invented that material deserves to be severely pistol whipped and left in the desert for dead. Maybe I'm a little too harsh. I suppose a moderate pistol whipping would do. The severe whipping is reserved for the jerk that invented corduroy. I can still hear the *io*whoosh *ic**io*whoosh*ic**io* *ic*those pants made as I walked down the hall. I think that's where spontaneous combustion comes from.

And, please, don't even get me started on white suits and the whole disco scene.

So, you see, I had experienced four or five different fashion epochs come and go in my short twenty years, so I wasn't too surprised to see that things were still changing. It was the way they changed that made my heart, among other things, go pitter patter.

I'm not sure what I expected to see. Maybe some kind of gossamer material that looked like it was made for fairies from spider webs. That wouldn't have shocked me too much. Some of the sci-fi movies showed people in the future wearing some kind of shiny material that looked like it would be at home in the fridge wrapped around leftovers instead of wrapped around someone's body.

The body. Yeah, that's another subject altogether and we'll get to that in a minute, or maybe two. In most of the movies about the future, most of the people had bodies that looked like they spent most of their time in the gym. Everyone in the future looked like Greek statues come to life, given a good tan, and buffed their complexion to a strong, healthy glow. Let's just say that the prophets of science fiction weren't far off the mark. If anything, they fell a little short of reality, but we'll get to that in a minute.

Jackee was a nurse. Now I know that uniform fashion changes. They don't change as fast or as drastically as the rest of the world, but everything changes eventually. The white dresses and stiff caps give way to tunics and smocks or something else along that line. I don't think I ever saw a nurse in tie-dye, but that's not to say that they don't exist. Most of the nurses I really remember are from my time in the military and all of them were in the same basic uniform as I was.

The memory is a funny thing. I remember clearly events in my life that I know never actually happened, even though I can give you details of what happened. So my memory of nurse's uniforms may be a little fuzzy, but one thing I know for sure is that they all had pockets, deep wide pockets for carrying lots of different things because nurses need a lot of different things. They need things like paper and pens. They needed tongue depressors and thermometers. They needed all kinds of things for all kinds of reasons and they needed pockets to carry those things.

Another thing I clearly remember is that those pockets were made out of some kind of material and that material usually matched what the rest of the uniform was made out of. So I guess in a way her uniform fit that criteria because her pockets were non-existent and so was the rest of her uniform. Nurse Jackee stood in front of me with her arms outstretched nude as the day she was born.

Now, as to the body. I won't describe it. I won't because I can't. Whatever I'd say about it would simply fall short of the truth of how beautiful, exquisite, magnificent, wonderful, and glorious,....I'm going to buy a thesaurus just so I can look up words to describe her. Imagine, if you can all the facets of the most beautiful women you've ever seen. The full round hips, the lustrous curves, you get the idea. Now take all the best from every woman, magnify it by a thousand and you still won't come close to how wonderful Jackee looked. And I looked like a reject from a zombie movie with my pasty white skin, disheveled hair, and pale comparison of what used to be a muscular physique, even if I did have hair on my chest.

"Come on," she urged. "Let's get you into the wheelchair and then into my car." At that point I could have floated to her car and then probably carried it to wherever she wanted to go.

"I guess I'm still a little wobbly on my knees," I

said as I leaned against her. Maybe I wasn't as wobbly as all that, but she wasn't going to know.

"That's to be expected," she assured me and directed me to the wheelchair. I thought about asking if I could lean against her some more and walk to the car, but as I turned toward the chair, I realized that some of that fake wobbling wasn't as fake as I thought. Even leaning on her, I don't think I could have walked another ten feet.

"Are we going to the hospital?" I asked. "For me to get checked out while I assimilate into society? Isn't that the way you put it?"

"Oh, no, Blue," she said. "You don't mind if I call you Blue, do you?" Call me red, green, or chartreuse, just call.

"Of course not," I told her.

"Good, and you call me Jackee. But we aren't going to the hospital. I'm taking you back to my place. I have all the equipment there to monitor your vital signs and you'll be much more comfortable there than in some clinical setting. It will be much easier for you to become used to your new surroundings. I have all the latest technology to help you recover the history you've lost for the last forty years and we can use that same technology to catch you up on music, movies, and other entertainment. Doesn't that sound better than some stuffy hospital room?" I had to agree that it did. Of course, I don't think any room she was in could be described as stuffy. She brought her own sunshine and fresh breeze of spring into any environment she was in.

"It sounds wonderful," I agreed enthusiastically. I hope I didn't sound too enthusiastic. I wasn't some teenage kid on his first crush. Then again, even though I was technically sixty years old, I wasn't too far from being a teenager with his first real crush, but I wouldn't admit that to her and I sure wasn't going to admit it to myself.

"Good, then it's settled," she said as she pushed me out of the facility that had been my home for the last forty years and into the bright sunshine. She handed me a pair of dark glasses. I don't even know where she pulled those from and I wasn't about to ask. Her car was sleek, sharp, and sophisticated. It looked like something from the future. I wouldn't have been surprised to see wings and have it fly.

"We won't be flying home today," she said as if reading my mind. "The drive will take about half an hour to my apartment. We'll get you a good shower, a hot meal, then tonight we'll have sex and in the morning I'll fix waffles. Sound good?" She might want to start taking my vital signs now, because I'm pretty sure my heart stopped beating.

"Excuse me," I managed to say.

"I said in the morning I'll fix waffles," she replied and helped me into the car.

Yeah, that cleared everything up just fine.

CHAPTER THREE

I stared back at what had been my home for the last forty years. It didn't look like much, but then it hadn't looked like much when I arrived either. NASA, in order to hide money I suppose, used the cover of a rundown VA hospital. It was a good cover, because no one wanted to go near those places, especially the veterans they were supposed to serve. I said it was a rundown facility, but come to think of it, I'm not sure it was any different from any other VA hospital, with the exception, of course, of Walter Reed. A hospital that serves Presidents, congressman, and other political operatives has to be first rate. As for the rest of us bums who merely fight and die so that politicians can be politicians, well, we get the leftovers, and there's not a whole lot of those to go around.

When I stopped staring at the hospital, I stared out at the landscape. It was bleak and desolate, like most of Texas, I suppose. I don't guess it's really fair to say that. I hadn't seen all of Texas, just enough to make me not want to see much more. In Arkansas, we had a joke about the best thing to come out of Texas. It was the I-10.

The landscape wasn't much too look at, but I kept gazing out there anyway because if I didn't, I was going to gaze at Jackee's body, and I had already done enough of that. She hadn't volunteered to put any clothes on, even when we went outside, and she hadn't volunteered to grab any clothes for me either. The vinyl seats were sticky and I was just a tad bit more self conscious than I was comfortable with. Suddenly the idea of a fig leaf felt very reassuring. The only thing covering either one of us was the seat belt across our shoulders and over our laps. Jackee said it was the law and that just made all kinds of sense to me. It was perfectly okay to display everything you had to the public, but you had to wear a seat belt in a car.

To pass the time, she turned on a video display of musicians from the eighties. I think it was her way of trying to make me feel comfortable while at the same time trying to bring me up to speed on how culture had changed over the years. I think she thought I might be impressed with how technology had evolved, but I was just a little underwhelmed.

The video screen was nice, especially since it was portable so you could take it with you on long trips. It sure would have come in handy when I was a kid on a field trip or travelling with a foster family. It sure beat the heck out playing license plate tag or I spy with my little eye. But in the end it was just a small television screen and they had been around for a long time. It was about time somebody had done something with them.

Then there was the cell phone she handed me. I guess folks need to get on each other's nerves a lot quicker now than they did when I was growing up.

She said it was good to have in case of an emergency, but Zeke had always taught me that the best thing to have in case of an emergency was a good dose of common sense. If you had enough of that, then you rarely had any emergencies. Besides, I remembered some of them characters on detective shows back in the seventies had car phones way back then. And wasn't a cell phone just one step up from that?

The thing I was least impressed with was something I couldn't even really see, and that was the internet. She said it was a great source of information, but it sounded to me like a place to lie your head off while safe at home in your living room. Or worse yet, pretending to be someone special when you were just really a frustrated bum still begging money from Dad while still nursing Mama. Boy, there was a visual I didn't need at the moment.

I decided to glance at some of the videos to distract my thoughts. It wasn't much help. The first one had some woman with the worst haircut ever singing about girls wanting to have fun. What girls should have been wanting was a barber who knew how to cut hair. Or maybe a lawyer to sue the barber who gave you that cut. I had a foster dad once who thought the only tools needed for a haircut was a pair of scissors and a bowl, and even he didn't give that bad of haircut.

The next lady sang about feeling like a virgin. One look at her and I knew she was singing about a long past memory. From the looks of her, it was a childhood memory, probably from before she was twelve, thirteen on the outside.

But it was the last one who really turned my stomach. It was the ugliest woman I had ever seen singing something about a coming chameleon. I don't know what a chameleon had to do with anything or why this ugly wench felt the need to sing about it, but it was really starting to get on my nerves. Then she sang a song asking if I really wanted to hurt her and I gotta be honest, I did. I wanted to punch her face in. I said something to Jackee about it and she just laughed. Guess it was an inside joke. You just had to be there. Anyway, her laughing made her body shake in ways I didn't need to see, so I turned back to the window.

I asked her to turn off the video so I could take time to absorb my new surroundings. Mostly I just wanted to think. It was kind of hard to do with all of the distractions. It was a wonder that any thinking got done at all with everything people had available to them. No one had to learn to read a map anymore since some woman named Suri told you where and when to turn. We had that when I was growing up. We called them back seat drivers and annoying.

Nobody had to learn much of anything at all, really. Anything you wanted to know was yours at the push of a button or the swipe of your finger. But mostly no one had to think much anymore and that was a real shame. I made my living in the Army doing just that. An analyst's job was to look at gathered information and then think on things for a spell before deciding what that information meant to people. I suppose nowadays people just plugged information into a computer and asked what it thought about things.

I thought about my activity in the capsule. I know, I was just lying there, so what kind of activity could I be recollecting on. Actually, despite the best theories of the scientists and others in the think tank that I found myself diving into, people in suspended animation still have brain activity. I don't know about any of the others who went through the process, but I dreamt, had thoughts, and even felt sensations around my body. There were times when I almost felt like I left my body, but I think that was just my own overactive imagination.

At first, the thing I enjoyed the most were the dreams. It was totally escapist, but when you're stuck in cocoon, escapism is a good thing. After awhile I realized that with just a little concentration I could tell when I was going into a dream state and sometimes even control the subject of the dreams. Yes, there were some sexual fantasies. I was twenty years old and facing forty years of isolation, of course there were fantasies of all kinds.

With a little more concentration I found that I could not only control the subject of the dream, but gradually, over time, control the destination of the dream. I began to concoct worlds within worlds. To be honest, it was intoxicating and more than a little addictive. Think about it. I was building entire worlds. That meant I was a creator. And if I was a creator, then in a way, I was the god of my own little world. For awhile, I hoped that the system would break down somehow and leave me there in my own little corner of the real world, because in that corner I was creating my own worlds where I was lord and master.

But then something happened. I got bored. Do gods get bored? I didn't know, but I knew I was and that was all the answer I needed. It was good in one way, though. It got me thinking about the real God. It made me wonder if there was one and if there was, what he was all about. Was he really the cruel tyrant people made him out to be? I looked forward to those times when I was in a semi-conscious state of mind and could do my deep thinking without drifting from there to dreamland. I found myself hoping that I would hear the Bible instead of one of the classics or some trashy romance novels. I had questions and I needed answers.

It reminded me of the questions I had when I was five of six and living with Zeke and Miss Martha. I gave a lot of thought to the times we went to church and the things I learned there. I remembered the preacher telling everyone that they needed to be saved. Saved from what, I didn't know. It seemed to me that most folks there had at least a decent life and weren't really in need of a rescue anytime soon. I remember him looking straight at me and telling me I needed to be saved. But again, from what?

I asked Miss Martha about it one Sunday evening. She said that people needed forgiveness for their sins. That didn't help much either. I was six years old when I got snatched away from them and I wasn't a perfect little angel, but at six you don't think much about sin. You think about snatching fireflies on a summer evening, taking walks in the woods, and finding a good swimming hole if you're lucky. Sin? That was something adults did.

Zeke wasn't much help either. He told me not to worry about it until I felt the Holy Spirit call me. God was going to call me? What if I wasn't home? Would God leave a message? Would he call back if I was out at the swimming hole when he called? We had a party line back then, so what if God called, and that old busy body up the road answered or at least listened in while God talked to me. I know that all sounds silly now, but when you're six, have questions, and those questions aren't answered, you come up with answers of your own and those answers usually lead to more questions.

Snug in my cocoon, the answers started coming to me. For one thing, it seemed that almost every time I was semi-conscious, it would be the Bible playing. I took that as a sign. Maybe it wasn't much of one. It might have just been coincidence, but somehow I kind of doubt. But whatever happened, it started answering questions for me.

For one, the thing I needed saving from was God himself. It seemed strange at first, since God was also doing the saving, but in the end it made sense. God is ticked. You don't hear that very often, but it's true. God is downright upset, and with good reason. Just about everything we do somehow messes up things for God. Even when we try to do good things, like feed the poor or build houses for homeless people, we do it for the wrong reason. We like to hear the attaboys. Thing is, only God really deserves any attaboys.

So God's ticked, but at the same time he loves us and likes hanging out with us. But we stink like a bunch of nasty pigs. That kind of stink don't come off easy. So who wants to hang around with stinking pigs? God does, only he has to clean up the stink first. So God sends his Son to die on the cross in order clean up our stink. But the stink has to go someplace. It's s a stink without a body. But when Jesus goes to the cross, He takes our stink and gives us his clean clothes to wear. It's a terrible swap, but God's happy with it. God's love and God's judgment meet right there where those two timbers meet on the cross, and that's right where Jesus' heart is.

So, laying there thinking about all the things I've done wrong, all the people I had hurt, all the times I could have done better, and I ask God to forgive me for all of it and to keep me away from any of the things that would take me back down that wrong road.

So here I am now, naked, in the car with a beautiful, blonde, blue-eyed, bronze skinned, naked woman, headed to her apartment where she wants to have sex with me. God has a sense of humor.

Don't get me wrong. I'm not a prude. Most times I just kind of live and let live and just do my best to get along in life. But fresh from talking to God about forgiving me for all my stink, I don't wanna step into another pile of it so soon. I figure I'll be stepping in it enough since it seems like the world is just full of it.

And there are parts of my body that say she offered, so we're two consenting adults. No foul, no harm right? I wish it were that easy, but that part of the body is south of the border. Zeke would tell me that God gave me two heads, but I'm only supposed to think with one of them. Problem with most folks is that they think with the little head and so only think little thoughts that get you in big trouble. He'd say something about one night of pleasure usually leads to a lifetime of problems.

Yu Hu found that out the hard way. No, honestly, that's his name. He was one of my friends from basic training. After basic, he went his way and I went mine. We got back together for the suspended animation project. He was going in for a year. Hopefully he would wake up a free man with an annulment. He told me the story before they put him in the cocoon.

During basic, he had met a beautiful Filipino girl while on a weekend pass. One thing led to another and six months later he gets a letter from her telling him he's gonna be a daddy soon. So Yu does the right thing and marries the gal. What a guy.

Only problem is, Yu is from Vietnam. She's from the Philippines. So how is it that his baby comes out as black as can be? Seems like God took a lot of different crayons out of the box for just one family and ain't none of them matching each other. That's when Yu started to contact lawyers.

Okay, so one body part is ready set go. My heart, on the other hand, is kind of tossing back and forth like a tennis ball. I love her. Or at least I think I do. She's beautiful, intelligent, charming, and she rescued me. What's not to love? Or maybe it's just that she's the first woman I've seen in forty years.

My head, to complicate things further, says put the brakes on and stop now before things get really complicated.

So one part says, "No, non, nein." Another part says, "Oui, si, ja." And still another part says, "je ne sais pas, ne se". So maybe the all the language lessons were paying off. I was now officially confused in four languages.

By the time we pulled into here parking space I

had my answer. I approached her as soon as we entered her apartment. It was a spacious place, well kept, and with a big couch that looked like it would be comfortable to sleep on. That was probably a good thing.

"Miss Jackee," I said nervously. I always resorted to a more polite way of talking when I got nervous. I found it set most people at ease and that helped set me at ease. "I sure am grateful for all you've done, but I was wondering if you could do me a favor."

"Miss Jackee," she said, arching an eyebrow. "Do I look like your mother?"

"No, m'am," I answered a little too quickly and forcefully.

"Mam?" The eyebrow arched higher.

"Sorry. I'm just a bit on edge. Anyways, I was hoping maybe you've got some clothes here for us to put on." I emphasized us. I wanted her to put something on more than I needed something.

"Don't you like what you see?" She asked, twirling about like a ballerina. Yes, yes I did like what I saw, which was the whole problem.

"Of course I do. It's just, well, a little distracting. Y'all may be used to running around like this," I said and waved my hands in front of myself, "but it's all a little new to me."

"I understand," she said, "but you might want to get used to the idea. Our creator made us in the beginning like this, and we're born like this, so this, so why should we fight against what our creator obviously wants for us. We only started wearing clothes out of shame, and since the prophet has come and told us our creator isn't ashamed of us, we don't need to be ashamed of our bodies anymore. Understand?" I shifted nervously. Part of what she said made a certain kind of sense. God did create us without clothes and we came into the world that way. But even though I couldn't quite put my finger on it, there was something a little off with her logic. Zeke would say that bird just wasn't gonna fly.

"I get it, but maybe you could just give me a little time to get used to the idea." She shrugged and that sure didn't help matters none for me. Then, she sighed and that was about to push me over the edge. Any resolve I had coming into the situation was washing away like a sand castle with the tide coming in.

"Okay," she said with a grin. "Be right back." A few minutes later she returned and I was sort of regretting asking her to put clothes on. It just seemed to make matters worse. She wore a large cotton t-shirt, cinched up tight around her very slim waist and thereby accenting her already ample curves. The hem was just long enough to conceal, but short enough that it made you want to peel it back. It was going to be a long night.

I got a similar t-shirt and a pair of shorts. I'm pretty sure she had shorts for herself too, but had no intention of wearing them. She had conceded as much territory as she was going to and in so doing had actually somehow gained some of my ground.

She fixed a small salad for herself and gave me a piece of clay with frosting on it that she called a protein bar. She said that after so long of not eating, it was probably all I could put on my stomach. I argued that what I really needed was a big, juicy, medium rare steak, but she insisted on the protein bar. I argued again that I was a growing boy and needed more on my stomach than one little snack. I ate more than that when I was still in diapers.

I ate half of it and almost threw up.

After dinner we sat on the couch. That's when I told her my decision.

"You are the most beautiful woman I have ever seen," I told her honestly. Miss Martha always said that adding a little sugar to medicine makes it go down a tad easier. I'm not sure, but I think she stole that thought from someone. I wouldn't dare to tell her that, but Zeke agreed with me, both on the theft of the line and on not sharing that information with Miss Martha. More than likely she would just claim that they heard her say it first and stole it from her.

"Why thank you, Blue," Jackee said. I think she actually blushed. How someone can walk around without a bit of clothes and not feel shame, but blush at a simple compliment is beyond me. Sixty years old and I still don't understand women.

"But I can't have sex with you tonight," I continued. "It's not that I don't want to.." I wasn't real sure how to approach this subject, but the direct way seemed best. She looked worried.

"I never thought about that," she said. "Is everything alright?" She asked as she was reaching for my shorts. I backed off quicker than a crawdad sensing a net.

"Yeah," I answered. "The plumbing is working just fine. That's not it. It's just that, well, there are other issues, personal issues, if you catch my drift." A sudden dawning of realization overtook her and she suddenly burst out laughing. I'm not sure what I said that was so doggone funny. I was trying to carry on a serious conversation, one of about ten I've had in my adult life, so maybe I said something funny and didn't realize it.

"I'm sorry," she finally said after catching her breath from all that laughter. "I never realized. I mean, we knew it was possible, but we assumed with you being in the Army and all, well, it just never occurred to us."

"Two questions. First, what never occurred to you. And second, what do you mean, us? Cause I know you ain't got no mouse in your pocket."

"Don't worry. It's fine now. I know back then you had to keep everything secret. That was even before the don't ask, don't tell policy. I'll call Bob. He saw your picture and was quite smitten, so I'm sure he wouldn't mind."

"Whoa!" I shouted and leaped off the couch. "Are you saying what I think you're saying? Are you asking if I'm queer?"

"We prefer the word, 'homosexual'. No one uses those aggressive words anymore. They're barbaric."

"You want to see barbaric?" I asked. "Get Bob anywhere near me and you'll see me get barbaric. I said the plumbing works, and I know a little bit about plumbing. For one thing, male pieces get inserted in female pieces. Common sense and common decency will tell you that much. But I'm beginning to think folks are in short supply of either of those here."

"Well, aren't you the intelligent one? Awake for a mere couple of hours and already you've figured out everything we're doing wrong."

I suppose I had gone a bit too far. I was a guest in her home after all, and she had offered me more than any man had a right to ask for, but I got a bit riled at the thought of being Bob's playmate. I needed to apologize, and quick.

"I'm sorry. I guess it's gonna take some getting used to being in this world. Things are so different.

For instance, no one would walk around without clothes. It just ain't proper. I know you explained about not feeling shame, but it's just so much different than what I'm used to." I started to relax and sit back down.

"I understand. I really do. And if you don't want to have sex, that's fine. We just thought that after forty years of sleep, you'd need a little release and I was more than willing..."

I was on my feet again, feeling just a little bit agitated.

"Wait a minute, wait just a doggone minute. Are you telling me I'm your pity sex? I ain't no one's pity sex!" I shouted.

"Blue, it's not like that. Things are different now. We love one another as our creator asks us to. So if someone has a need, then any one of us is willing to meet that need."

"Come again? I don't think I'm following you. In fact, I'm pretty sure I got lost right after 'things are different now'. What do you mean you love one another? I know the Bible says something loving one another, but I don't think that's what they had in mind?"

"And why not," she countered. "And I didn't say the Bible. That ancient book is part of the past and that's where it needs to stay...in the past. Think of it this way, if you were hungry and I had more food than I could eat, wouldn't I be wrong if I didn't share with you?"

"But we're not talking food here. We're talking about your body. You're comparing apples to oranges."

"Am I? Food and sex are just two basic needs. Why meet the one and not the other. No one is hurt by it and someone is helped. We live as if we are all one body, again as the creator asks. If one part of the body has a need, shouldn't the other parts see to that need?"

"What about disease?" I asked. "And pregnancy? Don't you worry about getting knocked up?" She laughed again. Not out of control like before, just a simple chuckle.

"There are no consequences for doing the right thing," she said. "All disease has been eradicated and we have one hundred percent foolproof birth control. So are you ready to take me to bed?" She asked coyly and began untying her sash. I was not feeling as strong as I wanted to. A lot of what she said made sense somehow. If everybody gave themselves like that, then where was the harm? And if everyone looked like Jackee, then I could see a whole lot of men wanting to take advantage of the situation. But if what she said were true, then in a way, there wouldn't be a situation to take advantage of because the girls would be just as ready as the guy. Still, somewhere in the back of my mind, there was a little voice that said something was rotten in Denmark. Just cause I couldn't find it doesn't mean it didn't exist. I wasn't sure if the voice was Miss Martha, Zeke, or someone else. I just knew I needed to get out of there fast if I was going to hold onto any form of morality.

"Maybe not tonight," I offered. "My stomach still ain't feeling the greatest and I don't think puking sounds very romantic."

"Romance has nothing to do with it," she said sourly. "It's just a basic need, but we'll wait until you feel more up to it. I'll show you the guest room where you'll be staying."

She showed me to a room just down the hall. It was small, with just room for a twin bed and a night stand. The bathroom was the next door down.

She gave me a peck on the cheek and told me I had no idea what I was missing. She probably was right. I was only twenty and my experience with women had been limited to necking and heavy petting. Yeah, I was twenty years old and a virgin. So what? Does that make me an alien from another planet or just a guy who thinks maybe there's a reason to keep sex special.

After she left, I did something I hadn't done since I was six and still with Miss Martha and Zeke. I bent my knees besides the bed and prayed. I hadn't talked to God since I had been taken from them two. I was too ticked to give him the time of day. Even after I thought I was over it, I still held back some anger just for God. After all, couldn't he have stopped it? Why let me go through all that pain? Why let the drunk live and take the only two people that had ever really cared for me? I still had all that anger just below the surface and tonight I finally told God about it. And I found out something that I had never known. Zeke had tried to tell me and I suppose Miss Martha had too, but I wouldn't listen to them. I was only six and I had the whole world, including God, all figured out. Or so I thought.

I found out there, beside the bed, that God was big enough to take my anger, pain frustration, disappointment, all of it and more, and still love me. I knelt there and cried for what seemed like hours, but was probably just a couple of minutes. Finally, I was ready to talk to God, and, more important, I was ready to listen.

"God," I started, "I don't know if what I did while in suspended animation meant much of anything. Technically, I was asleep. And I guess if you get right down to it, I might have been dreaming the whole dang time. Oops, don't know if it's okay to say dang. Dang, I said it again. Anyways, I wanted to ask again, forgive me for all the wrong I've done. I don't get it all. I'm pretty ignorant about most things, including the Bible, but I know Jesus died on the cross to pay for my sin. So I'm accepting that and asking you to accept me into Heaven.

God, I'm in a big pickle here. Jackee is a nice woman, and if you don't mind me saying, you sure did a good job putting her together. She's a sight to see. And to be honest, I enjoyed looking. Ain't no sense lying about it since you know better anyways. But, God, I'm trying to do the right thing and I could use a whole lot of help with that situation. Thanks."

I had been up for less than a half day after sleeping for forty years, but I lay down and was asleep before my head hit the pillow good. I didn't even dream.

CHAPTER FOUR

I woke up the next morning, took a shower, and found some folded clothes at the end of my bed. Change of pace? Oh well, whatever the occasion, I was glad to have some sense of normalcy returning to my world. Correction, their world. I was like Heinlein's character. I was a stranger in a strange time. After another quick prayer, I went out for what I hoped was bacon and eggs. It was, but not for me. I got the other half of the protein/clay bar from the night before. I guess sometimes when you pray for things, God just says no. I wondered if he might be laughing right now as I tried to choke down the rest of that brick. At least I got coffee with it. I tried soaking it in the coffee to soften it a little bit, but I think it just thickened the coffee.

Jackee was also dressed. She actually looked nice in a classy blue pantsuit that complemented, but didn't quite match her eyes. Yeah, we guys can notice things like that every now and then.

"You look nice this morning," I offered.

"As opposed to terrible last night, I suppose," she answered dryly. Sometimes, with women there isn't any winning. Okay, actually, you can't ever win with women, the best you can hope for is a draw. And that only rarely.

"You looked wonderful last night, too. It was just a little too much, a little too quick."

"I understand, Blue. I honestly do. But it does hurt a girl's feelings to be shut down like that." I felt terrible. I really did, but the alternative wouldn't have been any better. Okay, it would have been great for the fifteen minutes or so that it might have lasted, and since I was out of circulation for forty years, which was probably being generous, very generous.

We ate quietly. Well, she ate quietly. I crunched and munched and probably broke a tooth or two. I was just swallowing the last bite, along with a couple of molars when she broke the news to me.

"We'll be going to the hospital for some of your exams today."

"I thought you had all the equipment you needed here to take care of me and allow me time to assimilate back into society." I countered. I don't know why it upset me so much to go to the hospital. I had expected to go there right from the suspended animation. I thought it was probably written in stone someplace, or at least filed in triplicate in a bureaucrat's office. But when she took me home instead, I was not disappointed. It wasn't that I was afraid of hospitals. It's just that I associated them with dead people.

"After your outburst last night, I had no choice but to report your behavior. My superiors want a full psychological workup done on you. They think you might have aggressive tendencies."

"Let me save them the trouble," I said, "I was bounced in and out of at least a dozen foster homes. In two of those homes, the people who were supposed to be adults just wanted to have something to play with, and I was their new toy. When I wasn't in that kind of situation, I was in a group home where the only way to get what you really wanted was to fight for it. So, yeah, I can be a bit aggressive when called on." That was a whole lot more than I intended to say, but it felt good to get it off my chest.

"Wow, no wonder you feel so strongly about Bob. You probably associate him with some of your poor parental figures. I'm sure that after a few sessions with one of our doctors, you'll welcome some attention from Bob."

"I associate Bob with queer, abnormal, strange, and indecent and several other similar adjectives. And

I can talk to a hundred different doctors with thousands of sessions each and I'll still feel that same way." Her mouth was wide open in shock, but I wasn't about to change my mind on that subject. There were some things that were totally non-negotiable, and that was definitely on the top ten of that list.

"Well, that's what we need to see the doctors about. You know, if we can't at least convince you to accept that you might be wrong, it might mean sensitivity camp. Not many people want to go there."

"If it comes to me accepting that wrong is right, you might as well put me back in my cocoon and wake me up when the world has it's bearings again."

"You might need to consider that it's your bearings that are off," she offered. I had considered it for about fifteen seconds before deciding that idea needed to be crumpled up and thrown away with yesterday's stinking leftovers. I could accept a lot of things, even that people actually found that kind of behavior enjoyable. That was their business and I was fine with it as long they kept it their business. The problem was that they wanted to get their business all up in my business and that just wasn't going to fly.

About ten minutes later we were on our way to the hospital without another word. She knew by that time that I wasn't going to budge on that subject, at least not without large amounts of drugs and heavy doses of shock therapy, and even then I'd probably be electrocuted before they changed my feelings.

I looked out the window again, not because I was trying to avoid contact with her. Well, okay I was trying to avoid eye contact with her, but not for the same reason as yesterday. She had clothes on today. Today, however, I was more interested in my surroundings. I wanted to know what kind of world I had awakened to. I paid attention to the number of cars on the road, the height of and the ungodly amount of buildings there were, and especially the people, all the people. Most of them wore clothes. I was glad of that. I think Jackee had exaggerated their fascination with nudity. Although there were more than a few who wore nothing at all and quite a number of them whose outfits were actually more enticing than total nudity. It's funny how that works sometimes.

I also noticed that all of them looked fantastic. The guys all had bulging muscles and six pack abs, something I had only accomplished after eight weeks of basic training, and even then mine didn't look near as good as the ones I was seeing today. These were chiseled and hardened, as if cut from solid granite. Some of the women, though not many, shared that chiseled look. Others, most others, had flat stomachs, with just a little curve to the sides to give them some shape. All of them looked runway model ready. I felt like I had gotten dropped into the middle of a fashion show.

My mood was souring. It didn't start out the greatest, and the drive to the hospital wasn't helping. I was really hoping to spend the day with Jackee, to get to know who she was with her clothes on. I was really interested in her, not just her body. I wanted time to talk to her, find out her likes and dislikes, to look for common ground with her. I know that sounds kind of sappy, but I didn't have much of a track record with people in general and even less of one with women in particular. I guess you can blame it on moving around so much, having trust issues, or any number of the weeds that sprouted in my childhood, but the fact was I just didn't get along with people. I was a loner and most of the time, I liked it that way, but Jackee had changed that dynamic somehow. I really wanted to belong somewhere with someone.

Just ahead, I spotted something that looked like it might be a park of some kind. The buildings gave way to a clearing and I could see trees jutting up from the ground like ancient sentinels. The pavement gradually gave way to cobblestone and she slowed down the car accordingly. On the right I saw playground equipment. Real live playground equipment. Swings, slides, see-saws, the whole bit. I know for most people a simple park is not exactly the most exciting thing on a tourist trip, but for me, it was just this side of Heaven. Having missed out on most of my childhood, I sometimes lived it over through the eyes of those who were still in the midst of it. It was my arms swinging hand over hand on the monkey bars. It was my butt sliding down the slide. It was also my butt getting bounced up and down on the see-saw. I could sit and watch kids play for hours at a time. It was their innocence, their willingness to totally give into whatever activity they were doing, just for the fun of doing it. I loved their imaginations coming to life as they flew airplanes, drove tanks, or saved the princess from the giant gorilla at the top of the monkey bars.

I also loved to watch the eyes of the parents who were there to keep an eye on their little ones. It was wonderful to see someone care that much for someone else. I know there were a few times when I got the evil eye from a mom or two. And I didn't blame them. There I was, a grown man with no known attachment to any of the kids, watching a bunch of them play like I was some kind of pervert or something. It was only after meeting one of the mothers who had been a foster kid herself that I got the thumbs up to stick around, and only then with a probationary period. It was the only thing I had really missed when I went into my cocoon. Well, that and a good cheeseburger, but who doesn't miss a good cheeseburger with onions, lettuce, tomato and a whopping side order of fries?

"Slow down," I suggested. I wanted to see the kids playing for a little bit before we went for my examination. It might slow my heart down a little. As she slowed down, though, I saw something deeply disturbing. I was used to some making out going on in the park. Sometimes older siblings, who were supposed to be keeping their eyes on their young charges, only had eyes for each other. And who could blame them? Most of the time it was nothing more serious than some passionate kissing. Every once in awhile some of the parents even got a little carried away. I guess being in the vicinity of youthful innocence and young love brought out the amorous feelings even in older parents. So I wasn't too surprised to see some couples making out, but it was what I saw next that turned my stomach.

There were couples engaged in sexual activity not more than fifteen feet from where young children were playing. And as I looked closer, I saw that it wasn't just couples, but threesomes and foursomes, all of them participating in group sex orgies. I even saw people disengaging from one group, only to wander over to another group who looked a little more attractive, or who had something else going. I wasn't sure what was going on in their minds, and I didn't want to know.

I also saw bottles of wine and what looked like water pipes for smoking marijuana around some the crowds. And all of this within eyesight of children as young as toddlers.

"What on earth are they thinking?" I screamed. "Do they have any idea what they're doing? They're supposed to be protecting their children, not exposing them to that kind of sick behavior!" I yelled. I was beating on the glass, trying to get their attention. Trying to tell them to stop and think about what kind of thoughts they were putting in those young minds.

Jackee had locked the doors and also hit the window locks so I couldn't roll down my glass. I almost broke it in desperation.

"This is why we're taking you to see the doctors," she stated calmly. "This type of irrational thinking needs to stop."

"Oh, I agree." I said. "But it's not me that's thinking irrationally, it's the rest of the world. I used to hear people say stuff like that all the time, but it's finally true. I'm alright, it's the rest of the world that's crazy."

"The world is not crazy." Jackee retorted. "Children are going to be exposed to sexual behavior sooner or later and they'll need information so they can make good decisions about whether or not to engage in sex themselves when they're old enough."

"When they're old enough," I scoffed. "And just what is the age of consent in this brave new world, two or three?"

"Very funny," she said, but I didn't see much humor in any of it. "The age of consent happens to be twelve."

"And I'm sure that never gets violated. Does it?" She squirmed as I said it, and I knew it hit a nerve. "It does, doesn't it? You've got people who aren't satisfied with pre-teens, because that's too old for them."

"Parents can give consent for their children at times," she admitted reluctantly. "But it's a rare thing."

"How rare?" I asked.

"Okay, it's not a rare thing. It happens every day. It's not right, but it happens. And we aren't the ones to judge people. Some of them have very special needs."

"Like a bullet to the brain, or a scalpel to something lower," I stated flatly.

"That's the kind of talk that will get you in trouble," she warned.

"I don't care. That kind of stuff is sick and twisted and neither you nor any other doctor will ever convince me otherwise." They could lock me away if they wanted to, as long as I didn't have to see any more of this. But I had a couple of more questions that needed answered. I probably didn't want to hear the answers, but I was couldn't stop myself from asking the questions.

"Why would any parent allow that to be done to their child?" I asked. And then it hit me. "Money, right? It's always the poorer parents who are willing to sell the younger kids in order to put food on the table or to keep a roof over their heads. Isn't that right?"

She acknowledged that I was on the right course. No parent of means would ever sell or rent the consent for their child. In fact, most of their children were kept away in private schools until they were fifteen or older. It was hard to keep them from being sexually active after that time.

"How young?" I asked. I didn't want to know the answer. I knew that much, but I also knew I needed to hear the answer, no matter how badly I wanted to avoid it.

"Two is the youngest I've heard of, but I would imagine it goes lower," she admitted. I couldn't take any more. My mind was on serious overload and my heart felt like it was going to hammer itself right out of my chest. I needed to scream. I needed to run. I really needed to puke.

"Stop the car!" I demanded.

"We're almost there," she said. "The worst is behind us."

"Stop the car now, or get a lapful of vomit," I said. She stopped the car and unlocked my door. It flew open and I flew out, right onto my knees onto the sidewalk. And then I vomited. I threw up everything I had eaten, which wasn't much, but it didn't taste any better coming up than it did going down. Maybe, if possible, it was a little worse. I puked and I puked until even the dry heaves stopped. Then the tears came. Great floods of tears poured out of my soul, out of my eyes, and onto the puke strewn sidewalk. I wept for every innocent child I had ever seen or ever would see.

"I'm sorry," Jackee said, kneeling down next to me. "It may not seem right to you, but we want our kids to see sex it was meant to be, a beautiful thing."

"What I just saw was not beautiful. And don't try to sell me that load of crap about teaching children about the beauty of sex. What you're doing is desensitizing them to it so you'll be able to lower the age of consent. We used to do something similar to our soldiers going into combat."

"What do you mean?" She asked.

"We would have our soldiers watch hours upon hours of violent atrocities. Stuff that would sicken the normal man. And it did, too. It sickened all of us, but then something strange happened."

"What?" She wanted to know, genuinely interested.

"First, we got used to it. Then, we accepted it. And then, we started to enjoy it. We looked forward to the mutilations and dismemberments. We started cat calling and wanting more. That's when our supervisors knew we could go into combat situations and shoot without hesitation. It wasn't pretty." Tears had started down her cheeks as well, not many, but enough to let me know that somewhere in there was still human after all.

"We need to go," she said, standing and drying her eyes. She turned sharply from me and strode back to the car. Somehow I regained my composure and followed her, but my mood had definitely gone from bad to worse to homicidal. Given half the chance, I would probably kill the next pervert I saw. I felt like Dorothy, only in my new world the lion, the witch, and the wizard was all together for a magical orgy. Shoot, the dog might have been in there too. It sure wouldn't surprise me.

When we got to the hospital, I growled at anyone that looked sideways at me, which turned out to be most people. I was the new kid in town. I knew how that felt. I had been in the same situation all too often as a kid. The best thing to do then was find the biggest and baddest bully I could and just stomp the snot out of him before he knew what was coming. Nine out of ten times I could do exactly that. In Arkansas in the nineteen sixties, it wasn't just the white people who could be prejudiced. Zeke and Martha welcomed me into their homes and most of the other folks welcomed me into their community, but not everyone was so friendly. So I had to learn to fight, run, or die early on in life. I guess I was a little lazy, because running seemed like too much work and I wasn't ready to die just yet.

I was poked, prodded, and pierced. They drew enough blood for an all you can eat vampire buffet. They also swabbed my mouth with a q-tip, took urine, hair, and nail samples, and wanted me to give a fecal sample, but I had vomited the only food I had eaten, so it was a no go. The nurses were all friendly and all of them had bodies similar to Jackee's, well endowed with slim waists and flawless complexions. I was about to get sick of it. I would just about kill for someone with a pimple and maybe a little bit of a love handle. Would it hurt them to at least try to look like normal human beings?

My last hurdle before going home was an appointment with the counselor, Dr Frank Guinness. What they meant to say was I was supposed to get cleared by the local shrink, but they were way too polite for that. Something about seeing a psychiatrist might affect my self-esteem and make me cry and curl up in a ball or something. I really did need a tissue because there were a lot of butt wipe pansies running around who needed their backsides wiped. I was in the bathroom washing up when I saw what I assumed was an orderly or something primping in front of the mirror. After what I had seen earlier, I was feeling a bit surly.

"Nice job covering that bald spot in the back," I said as I walked past. I saw him a little later, curled up on a couch in the waiting area, rocking back and forth sobbing. There were a couple of people gathered around him trying to comfort him. It was pathetic. I caught the eye of one of the ladies with him and she tried to stare a hole through my heart.

"Good luck with that, sweetheart," I thought.

"Better than you have tried."

"Let's get you into the counselor before you cause a mass suicide epidemic." It was Jackee, tugging at my arm and pulling me away from the pathetic loser on the couch.

"Boo hoo," I said passing by.

"Stop it!" Jackee demanded. I just couldn't.

She walked me down the hall at a quick trot, trying to keep me from hurting anyone else's feelings, I suppose. She didn't let go of my arm until she was pushing me through the door marked "Dr Frank Guinness, Counselor". I was going to puke again.

"Come in," said a sultry voice. I could only assume it came from the good doctor's secretary or nurse, because people named Frank don't have voices like that. I was wrong. At this point, I'm not sure whether to introduce Dr Frank as a man, woman, or something in between. He/she was sitting behind a desk, wearing a formal gown that looked like it came straight from a debutante's ball. If that is, the ball was held in honor of the East German ladies Olympic team.

"This is going to be a nightmare," I said and stuck my hand out for a handshake. For a minute, I thought he/she was going to turn it over and kiss it. Fortunately, a firm handshake was all I got.

"Why do you say that?"

"No reason," I lied. "I don't suppose you know a song about a chameleon?"

"No," she purred. Yeah, it actually purred. I was really going to throw up again. Either that or I was going to throw a hard right.

"Look, I don't know what the point of this is, but I think I should just be going."

"You don't think I can help you with your aggression?"

"I don't think you can help anyone until you get help for your own problem," I answered honestly. "I stopped playing dress up when I was about eight or nine, and then I was dressing up as a cowboy, not a ballerina."

"Oh, you are a bad one," the good doctor said. "I was given this body by our creator, but in my heart, I feel more like a woman, so I dress as one. Is that so wrong?"

"On your own time, I don't care if you dress like a sea monster, but since I'm being forced to talk to someone, I prefer someone with a good foothold in reality."

"Just because I identify as a woman doesn't mean I don't have a grip on reality," the doctor countered. "In fact, I am willing to accept who I am despite appearances to the contrary. I would think that shows that I have a better grip on reality than you, Mr. Blue."

"Let me get this straight," I said, "you think that because you're willing to live in a fantasy world and want to drag me along into it, kicking and screaming I might add, you have a better grip on what's real than I do. You're thinking is as twisted as your bra strap, doc."

"No need for aggression," the doctor stated.

"Who's being aggressive?" I asked.

"You," Dr. Frank answered. "Your body language, your words, your whole attitude screams aggression."

"If I scream anything," I said, "it's going to be that the nuts are running the asylum. The adults are acting like children, and the children are exposed to sexual deviancy so they can supposedly prepare for adulthood. Now what part of this topsy turvy world makes sense to you, doc?"

"All of it," Dr. Frank said. "I've been watching you on closed circuit television. You are a bully and you've been pushing your view of morality on everyone since you've arrived. Who are you to say what is right and what is wrong? We are not to judge anyone."

"But there you are judging me," I stated. "How does that work?"

"I am not judging you, Mr. Blue. I'm merely pointing out your misconceptions about society. One cannot go through life without facing the harsh reality of his choices."

"You sit there pretending to be a woman when you're obviously a man, and want to lecture me about facing reality?" I was dumbstruck. This conversation was just about to come to a quick conclusion and I was going to find a charbroiled double cheeseburger with either fries or onion rings, maybe both.

"I choose to be a woman, therefore I am a woman," the man who was not a woman said. "Now let's get to your problems."

"Here's my problem, doc, I think I'm a dog. I really do. I identify as a half Dachshund and half Poodle. I guess that makes me a Doodle."

"Now you're just being facetious," Dr Frank said, a bit irritated.

"No, seriously, I really have this urge it take a big dump all over your carpet, mark my territory all around the room and then hump your leg. What would you do if I give into my compulsions?"

"You know very well what I'd do. I'd have the orderlies come in and restrain you."

"But why?" I asked innocently.

"Because obviously you'd be showing a break with reality," Dr Frank answered.

"And yet you don't see the irony in any of that, do you, doc?" I asked. Then said, "This session is over, doc. Call my secretary and have her set up your next appointment. I think we're making real progress here." With that, I turned around and left the room under the protesting voice of Dr Frank Guinness.

"How'd it go?" Jackee asked.

"Fine," I lied. "Now let's get out of here before I beat someone to a pulp." I strode out of the parking lot, barely letting her catch up before I got to the car. "Let's go somewhere and get a cheeseburger."

"Gross," she exclaimed. "You actually eat dead meat?"

"Well, I prefer it alive, but it howls when I bite into it and the fur gets stuck in my teeth. A man has to face his limitations."

"Fine, I guess. But you'll have to eat it there by yourself. I'm not going to sit there and watch you gorge yourself on some poor defenseless beast."

"Poor defenseless beast?" I asked incredulous. "I ain't talking about clubbing baby seals. Burgers are made from cows. You know, big lumbering creatures that weigh a ton and sometimes have horns. They ain't the smartest animals, but hardly defenseless."

"Raised for nothing more than to be slaughtered so you can feed yourself? How do you sleep at night?"

"On my side, usually," I quipped. "But I roll over occasionally."

"How would you like to be a cow?" She asked.

"Hmm..." I pondered, "fed as much as I could eat, kept out of the elements, given proper medicine and care. Not a bad life."

"Until you're slaughtered."

"We all gotta go sometime," I answered.

"And how would you like it if people ate you when you died?" She wanted to know.

"Fine by me," I told her. "But I gotta warn you, I'm full of bone and gristly. I probably don't taste good either."

Despite her objections, we found a fast food restaurant that still served all beef patties on a bun with lettuce, tomatoes, and onions. I was in paradise. I ate every bit of it, all of the fries, and even licked the excess salt off of the wrapper. I washed it all down with a large soda.

"I hope it makes you ill," she said.

"Tsk, tsk," I replied. "You shouldn't be so aggressive and judgmental. Perhaps we should make an appointment with Dr Frank for you. The two of you could go shoe shopping together and talk about proper make up applications while he works on your aggressive impulses.

Needless to say, she wasn't amused. We drove home in silence. As soon as we got home, she went straight to her bedroom, leaving me alone, which was fine by me. I took a long hot shower, brushed the rest of that delicious burger from between my teeth, and bent over the bed to talk with God about my day. It was an interesting, if one sided conversation.

CHAPTER FIVE

Jackee had told me that she had a line of credit with the local supermarket, so I woke up extra early and decided to make good use of it. I walked down to the place she had pointed out in our drive to the hospital the day before and went in to buy some decent breakfast food. I knew Jackee objected to eating "dead animal flesh" as she called it, so as a good guest in her home, I decided against the bacon and sausage. I'd have to find a job soon so I could afford my own place and start living by my own set of rules, which included eating dead animal flesh. But it was only my third day in this society and I was pretty sure there wasn't a lot of call for a forty year old skill set. Still, I had a strong back and a weak mind, two variables needed for doing manual labor. I wasn't looking to get wealthy, just to get by.

I rounded up eggs, soy sausage, hash browns, orange juice and milk. I'd have to find a job soon or I'd up in debtor's prison. I couldn't believe the cost of everything. That kind of money would have filled up two shopping carts at least. Okay, maybe not two, but one very well rounded over.

On the way back to the apartment, carrying my breakfast in a small tote, I began to think about what my life here would be like. I had already decided to look for work. That much was a given. I really appreciated all that Jackee had done for me, but I wasn't meant to be a kept man. I needed to find my own way in the world, and I couldn't do that waiting for handouts from beautiful women. Besides, I liked her. I mean, I really liked her. And no self respecting man could ask a woman out on date and then expect her to pay for it. Oh, it happened. Every so often, some worthless wimp of a man asked a girl to pay for dinner and a movie, and probably still expected her to put out later. It happened, but it wouldn't be happening with me.

I noticed a sign hanging in a window just a block from the apartment. It was another apartment for rent. I peeked inside. It wasn't bad. A little small, I suppose, but it was plenty big for a single guy like myself. I know, I had to find a job first, but it didn't hurt to take a look. It would give me a goal to work towards. I was hungry and Jackee would be waking up soon and wondering where I was. I should have left a note. I didn't expect to be gone long, but I really wanted to take a look inside. Just a short look and then I'd be on my way back to the kitchen.

I wasn't disappointed. It had both a stove and a fridge, both old, but still working. The bedroom was in the back, away from the noise of the street. The only drawback for me was that it was a basement apartment, which meant it was easier to break into, but there bars on the windows and the door had a good deadbolt. Besides, what did I have that anyone would want to steal.

I made my way back to the apartment whistling a merry tune. Okay, it was more like humming since I never learned to whistle, and it was more or less an old rock ballad I could only remember about half the words of, but I hummed it with a smile on my face.

That smile was still on my face as I approached the apartment building. Despite the electronic stimulation I received while asleep, all of my muscles had atrophied horribly. I wasn't ready for a marathon before. Okay, I could have finished one, I just wouldn't have come in the top ten. But now I was feeling the strain after just a couple of blocks of brisk walking. I was going to have to get myself back into top physical condition. And even then, I wouldn't be able to compete with the walking Michelangelo statues that seemed to be everywhere. Have I mentioned that I was getting sick to death of physical perfection, and that on both men and women? Believe me, there is something to be said for too much of a good thing.

Anyway, I needed to be in as good as shape as I could. The only person I was really competing with was myself so I was the only one I needed to worry about. Keeping your nose in your own business is the best way to keep it from getting chopped off. So I decided to skip the elevator and walk the five flights of stairs. It wasn't a marathon, but it was a start.

Somewhere between the third and fourth floor was almost a finish. My heart was racing, my head was pounding and my breath was coming in shallow gasps. But there was more at work than normal exertion. I know, I'm just making excuses for myself, but, no, really, there was something happening I couldn't explain. I started feeling light headed, and then kind of muddle headed. I'm not for sure that there is such a word as muddle headed, but it's one of them phrases I grew up with and that's good enough for me.

So there I was, panting like a St. Bernard on a hot summer day, my chest beating like Ricky Ricardo's bongos, and I find myself muddle headed. I trudged along, commanding myself to just put one foot in front of the other. One step, two steps, three steps. It was like walking through lime jell-o. Okay, I don't really know what it feels like to walk through Jell-o, and even if I did, why would it have to be lime? I don't know, but it's how I felt at the time. By the time

I reached the apartment, I was soaked through with sweat. I pulled my shirt off as soon as I entered the apartment, dropping it off in the basket in the bathroom before washing my hands so I could properly prepare breakfast.

Making breakfast was not as easy as it seemed. I'm no Julia Child or even a galloping gourmet. I can fry an egg, make pancakes, and fry bacon without having strips of charcoal. Beyond that my culinary skills are minimal. I wouldn't starve to death if I had to eat my own cooking, but there might be times I'd wish I could. I once made oatmeal that was used as mortar to repair some loose bricks in the mess hall. Well, it might not have been that bad, but our commanding officer told me to stop making oatmeal before I killed myself or someone else it might have fallen on.

Still, I managed to fry some eggs, cook the soy product that was suffering an identity crisis, thinking mistakenly that it was sausage, and even managed to pop some toast in the toaster. I was buttering the toast when Jackee walked out of her bedroom She was absolutely radiant, wearing a sheer top that revealed almost everything without revealing anything. Sounds weird, I know, but I was there.

Now, I'm not the sharpest tool in the shed. And I'm not the kind of guy who notices every little thing a woman does. Besides, I was almost recovered from my Jell-o walk, but the muddle head was still attached to my muddle shoulders, so I don't really blame myself for not seeing what was obvious right at first. Okay, it wasn't at second or third either. It was somewhere in the upper teens before I saw what was in front of my eyes the whole morning.

"Happy anniversary!" She gushed. Okay, it had been a day. It wasn't exactly a milestone in our relationship, but I was willing to play along. Besides, I was feeling kind of rotten for some of the things I said and did at the hospital the day before. I meant everything, but there are times when you can speak the truth and make needless enemies or just keep your big trap shut and do yourself no harm. Somebody said something about being quiet and thought a fool or opening your pie hole and letting everybody know there ain't no doubt. I was in the no doubt about it category yesterday. I embarrassed the only friend I had, and had alienated a whole lot of people who might be my boss one day. For all I know, one of them could live in the same apartment building as Jackee's or even own the whole danged building. The point is I had to starting controlling my tongue before I ended up in real trouble.

"Breakfast is almost ready," I announced proudly. Hey, I had managed to cook without causing the fire department to be called out, or poison control. For me, that was a just shy of graduating from culinary school.

"Aw," she said. It was more like, "Awwwww," but you get the point.

There was something different about her. I could see it, and yet totally miss it at the same time. It was like one of those puzzle pictures that served as the cover for one of my favorite magazines. You had to find the thing that didn't fit in. Of course, in the mind of a four or five year old, everything fit in. It was just a matter of your imagination.

But this wasn't my imagination. There was definitely something different about her. I just couldn't quite put my finger on it. I think part of the problem was that my head still had not cleared from the Jell-o walk I had taken earlier. Everything was just a little fuzzy. In a way, it was like new memories were lying in over the old, but it was more like recording on a cassette tape, especially one of the cheap ones. The stuff you had recorded on there earlier would bleed through what you had just recorded, causing a lot of distortion. Okay, if you've ever recorded a favorite song from the radio on a cassette tape, and then heard a new favorite song that you liked more and recorded over the earlier one, only to have some weird, freaky hybrid of the two play back, then you know what it was like in my head. Not pretty, but Jackee sure was. I mean even prettier than I remembered. It was part of the overall something different thing.

The first thing I noticed was her breasts. Yeah, I know, that's the first thing every guy sees. It's not our fault, really. No, really, it's not our fault. It's Newton's fault. No, not the fig guy. I'm talking about the one who made up the rules about gravity. The bigger something is, the more gravitational pull it has. So while eyes are about the size of, let's say Mercury, the breasts are more like Jupiter. I know, you thought I was going to say Uranus. That's a joke for another day.

But this morning, they were more like Jupiter plus a couple of moons. I don't really understand how, but they were even bigger than I remembered, which was weird, since I just saw them yesterday. But there they were, larger than life, or at least larger than I remembered them being. Bigger, fuller, firmer maybe. I could only guess on that last one. Made me think of that television show. "We can rebuild them, make them stronger, faster..... better than before."

Or something like that.

Then there was her complexion. It had been flawless the first moment I saw her, and I didn't think you could improve on flawless. It wasn't just make-up. In fact, I don't think she was wearing any. But she had a glow about her. A glow that radiated from somewhere deep inside. It was gorgeous, like the sunrise on a beach. There I was getting all poetic.

Then it hit me. No, it literally hit me. She came up behind me while I was flipping the eggs and kissed me on the back of the neck, sending shivers down my spine. I convulsed slightly from the shivers and backed up into her. That's when I felt the bump. Okay, so it didn't hit me. I hit it. Technicality.

"What's that?" I said, turning around and looking down at the protrusion from her belly. She was either pregnant or in this world you could eat a watermelon seed and end up with a melon in your belly.

"Who's that?" She said. "And the answer is your son. Are you alright? You look a little out of sorts."

"How did that happen?" I asked, incredulous.

"Don't you mean, when? I mean, it could have been in the bedroom. You know we kept that place busy. Then there's the sofa, the couch, and the recliner. Sometimes all in one night, you naught boy."

"But," I started to protest. I couldn't remember anything about what she was talking about. I couldn't remember a single time that I had done anymore than allow my imagination to wander a little too far. She had wanted to that first night, but I had declined. What was I thinking? Never mind, I knew exactly what I was thinking. I was thinking that I had been changed during my long sleep, and that I had an encounter with God. That kind of encounter changes people. It had changed me, because the guy I was entering that chamber would have jumped at the chance to bed a beautiful woman like this. I had dreamed of encountering such a woman. But that was the old me. The new me said no and meant no. So at what point had the new me reverted back to the old me, and how did it all happen in one night?

Wait a minute! Women don't get big, fat pregnant

overnight. I'm pretty sure that even with instant oats, minute rice, and microwaves, some things still take time. Unless, of course, I had wandered aimlessly into a horror movie and she was about to explode out with a vampire/werewolf hybrid that had been implanted in her by space aliens. Okay, even for me, that was a little weird. That cassette tape was rewinding in my head again, playing memories that were there, then weren't. Others were slowly, but surely, being recorded over them, causing an awful lot of weird distortion in my head. It was time for two aspirin and call the doctor in the morning. And right on cue.....

"I think we should call Dr. Frank," she suggested. "He said there might be days like this."

"Yeah, my momma said there'd be days like this, too. She also said you can't hurry love, and you'd better shop around. But we're not calling her either."

"You can't remember the past year and a half, and you want to make jokes about it?"

"I'm sorry. It's the way I handle stress sometimes. I'm not sure what's wrong. I was fine when I woke up, or at least I think I was. I went to the store, stopped by an apartment I saw for rent on the way home, then kind of got a little dizzy taking the stairs up, but other than that I've been fine." That was the morning in a nutshell. I was fine until I took those stairs. Maybe I suffered a stroke or something. My body thought it was only twenty, but technically it was around sixty. I guess on average I was forty. Still, I wasn't in bad

shape for a forty, twenty, or sixty year old man,
certainly not bad enough to be having strokes,
blackout spells, or whatever else was causing my
confusion.

"Was it the cute basement apartment about a
block from here?" She asked. I told her it was. "You
rented that almost a year ago. You said you didn't
want to be a kept man."

"Wait a minute," I said, "you're carrying my baby
and we're not married? I'm living in my own
apartment."

"First of all, you spend most of your time here.
You got the place so you could have some private
time to relax and unwind. And second, no we're not
married. I explained that to you when I told you about
the baby. No one gets married. The creator told us
we're to be like the angels in Heaven, not marrying or
giving in marriage. We give to everyone who asks,
sharing our bodies with one another the way our
creator tells us to. Marriage promotes jealousy, rage,
and envy."

I was pretty sure that at any minute a white rabbit
with a top hat was going to run through the apartment
yelling, "I'm late, I'm late..."

Breakfast was getting cold, which was alright
because in all the confusion, my appetite had run off
with my brain. If you see either one of them, would
you mind asking them to come home, or at least call

to let me know they're okay.

"I could show you again how we made Junior," she offered teasingly, approaching me with a come on smile and reaching her hands around my waist. She pulled me in close and I felt "Junior" rub against me. I was really a daddy, or at least I was going to be in about three months. She did tell me she was sixth months along, hadn't she? If she didn't, how did I know about it? I was about to give in to her tempting offer. After all, why not? I obviously had already given in at least once before. According to her, probably thousands of times before, in every place and at every time imaginable.

"Might help jog my memory," I agreed, pulling her in tighter. Suddenly, she pulled back away from me, slipping away from my grip and traipsing down the hall to the bathroom?

"Just remembered, it will have to wait. It's Creator's day. We need to get ready."

"Creator's day?" I asked, having no idea what she was talking about.

"Don't tell me you've forgotten that too? I could maybe forgive you for not remembering us and our baby. Maybe. But to forget giving praise and honor to our creator? We have to call Dr Frank first thing in the morning." She wasn't angry. Not yet, anyway, but she was real close and definitely hurt by my amnesia or blackouts or whatever was happening.

"So it's church," I offered, trying to be helpful. I've got a word of advice for the guys out there. When you are already in trouble, don't say anything to try to get yourself out of it and don't, under any circumstances, try to help unless you absolutely know what you're doing. I didn't.

"Church?" She said it like it was a curse word. I just knew she was going to grab my ear, haul me off to the bathroom and wash my mouth out with soap.

"Uh, yeah," I said, digging my grave just a little bit deeper.

"Every church was closed years ago. All churches do is promote ignorance, fear, anger, and violence. Why would anyone want to go to church?" She was passionate and fiery. I don't know where she had gone to church, but the closest thing to violence I had seen in church was a couple of people arguing over the last chicken leg.

"Okay, so not church," I said. "Then what?"

"The sanctuary," she said with a serene look. "We praise our creator at the sanctuary."

"So we worship God, not at church, but at the sanctuary." I offered, trying to sum up and clear the muddy water I had been stirring. Instead, I threw in another shovel full of mud.

"Not God, the creator. And we don't worship him,

we worship he who is to come after. The creator is not a god, he is a man," she said, as if beginning a chant. That chant was answered by someone coming through the door.

"He is a man, but more than a man."

"More than a man," she answered back, "but just a man."

"He is a man," the voice echoed, "but more than a man." Man, oh man, I was about to get sick. The voice belonged to Bob, her homosexual friend that she suggested might want to have sex with me, which I promptly denied any aspiration to that regard.

How did I know it was Bob? Had I met Bob? She had only mentioned him once, hadn't she? There was that tape again in my mind, rewinding, recording, rewinding some more, and then recording another song over the first. I knew Bob. We had met. I think. I don't know. Maybe we had and maybe he was just a figment of my imagination. It was really getting harder and harder to tell. By this time, I didn't know whether to drink the stuff to make me smaller, or the stuff to make me grow taller. I didn't even drink, but at that point I might have taken it up.

"You kids better hurry," Bob stated. "The celebration begins in just over an hour."

"That's plenty of time," Jackee argued. Then, to me, "Go shower and put on the tunic I laid out on your bed. Hurry, please." I had been in the military. I could shower and shave and be inspection ready in less than ten minutes. This time it took seven, but only because she had moved my sandals. Yeah, I said sandals. I had a hard time getting those since most of the time everyone walked the streets nude, often engaging one another in intercourse. Jackee told me that I'd need to make up my mind soon about whether or not I was going to be a true member of society since I had refused several offers from women and almost punched a guy for offering. I probably would have punched him or worse if Jackee hadn't restrained me. I noticed Bob didn't offer, which was good because I would hate to have to hurt someone on Creator's day, or whatever the holiday was.

We took Bob's car, a stretch limousine with every amenity imaginable, and some I hadn't imagined. The streets were crowded with, I suppose, all the others who were headed to their sanctuary for Creator's Day. I supposed that everyone had their own sanctuary to go to since even the larger churches of my day couldn't hold this many people. I'm not sure if some of the sports arenas could hold the crowd I seen gathering together.

The sanctuary we attended was more like a large warehouse rather than any church I had attended. There was a large raised platform in the middle that I suppose could be used for a stage. On closer look, that's exactly what it was. There were musical instruments set in the middle and column speakers on each corner. Well, at least we'd have some entertainment.

We had only been there a couple of minutes when the excitement began. The lights dimmed, then exploded in a frenzy of pyrotechnics and noise. The band took the stage. I'm still not sure where they came from. I guess some kind of trap door set up under the stage. They played a hard pounding rendition of something that was vaguely familiar, but I couldn't remember why. The crowd was going wild. They were swaying, jumping, and I guess dancing, but it looked wild and frenetic, like they were caught more in a trance rather than in control of their own bodies. Then the music stopped abruptly. The lights dimmed. And then the voice spoke.

"My brothers and sisters.....welcome! Welcome to Creator's Day, my creations!"

"The creator is not a god, he is a man," one side began.

"He is a man, but more than a man," the other side answered back.

"More than a man, but just a man," came the reply.

"He is a man, but more than a man," said the echo. This went on for what I'm sure was about five minutes, but felt like five weeks, months, years. The crowd was softly swaying now. Rhythmically swaying back and forth like wheat on a Kansas field caught in a crosswind.

"In the beginning," the creator said, "God created the Heavens and the earth."

"So far, so good," I thought.

Garden scenes were projected on the walls. Idyllic, pastoral scenes of what I guessed were supposed to be the Garden of Eden. A man and woman appeared on the scene, Adam and Eve, of course. And of course, they were totally nude and totally hot. It wasn't like the flannel board scenes in Sunday school where leaves, bushes and other camouflage to hide certain parts of their bodies. Everything was in view here.

"But the man and woman needed a test to define their love. They needed to experience freedom. Without it they would never leave the garden and fulfill God's purpose for their creation." The scene shifted slightly, showing Adam and Eve in various states of repose, relaxing in the Garden. They were downright slothful. No wonder God wanted them out.

It wasn't exactly the way I had thought of it, but it might have worked out that. I thought they did something worthwhile in the Garden. I wasn't sure what they were doing, but I didn't think they just crashed and burned on God's dime. That's the way it looked on the visuals, which were persuasive, much more than flannel board had ever been.

"So Lucifer, that great Archangel, volunteered to put them to the test. He showed them a path of enlightenment which opened the rest of the world to their eyes. They now saw everything that God had offered them, not just the Garden, but the whole world. But after leaving their home, they rebelled against God and began clothing themselves, becoming selfish with their bodies. They stopped giving themselves to each other and began to enforce man made rules of morality. Rules against homosexuality. Rules against sexual intercourse outside of the man made institution of marriage."

Okay, that was nothing like I remembered. Not even close. Where was the apple? Or pear? Or banana? Or whatever fruit it was supposed to be? And what happened to Satan and the serpent? Where were the forbidden tree and Adam and Eve hiding themselves because they knew they were naked and ashamed? I don't know where this guy went to Sunday school, but it wasn't the same place I went. I don't think even the far out churches taught anything like this.

"They covered their bodies with clothing, killing animals to do so. They shed the blood of innocents to cover themselves. Selfish beings. So God cursed them with fat and cellulite. He cursed their beauty and it became ugliness. He cursed their perfection and it began to decay and rot. He cursed all of the earth for the sake of man, who elevated themselves above the animals. And that curse reigned for thousands of years, until Lucifer sent forth his prophet to release man from the curse."

Okay, I know my theology isn't the best in the world, but I do know who the good guys are and who the bad guys are. And Lucifer ain't one of the good guys. And he doesn't send out prophets, well maybe false prophets, but not the real thing. This was all sick and twisted, and yet, somehow, with the confusion of my own head still holding sway, it began to make sense. It was the calm voice, the visual scenes that played out with the narration, the lights brightening and dimming, the music had begun again at some point. It was an audio/visual hallucination.

"Our bodies have been released from that curse. We no longer have to cover our bodies. Our bodies are as close to perfection as they will be until our lord comes to save us from this cursed planet."

Sometime during the speech, people had begun stripping off what little clothing they had on. Shirts, shorts, various undergarments, even socks, began piling up near the stage as if it were an offering to the creator. And sure enough, with a flash of light and a puff of smoke, the creator was there on stage. It had to be the creator. I had seen a lot of different men since awakening, and all of them in pristine shape, but they were ninety eight pound weaklings getting sand kicked in their face compared to this guy. He had to be about six foot eight or nine and close to three hundred pounds, all of it with no fat and a slim, trim waist. He made every other man look small and insignificant in comparison. Several women who were near the stage fainted. So did a couple of guys. It was downright embarrassing.

"The curse has been lifted," he called again, "give yourselves one to another in honor of our God." And they did exactly that. People started breaking off in couples, trios, and groups with more people than I could count since all I could see was a mass of arms, legs, and torsos. I felt myself being groped and pulled. I felt totally out of place since not only was I not engaging in intercourse, but I was still fully dressed, right down to my sandals. I began looking for a way out of there.

I made my way to where I thought the door was, bumping into nude bodies along the way. No one seemed to mind. They were too caught up in their frenzied behavior. It was more than my mind could handle. I was about to explode into a full blown panic. And that's when I noticed the smoke coming out of the vents. On top of everything else I was experiencing, now the place was on fire. I started to cry out in alarm, shouting warnings to whoever would listen, which wasn't very many people.

"Cool it, man," one man finally told me. "That's the gift our Creator. He gives us his very breath to take in as our own." And as if on cue, the voice of the creator was back.

"Breathe, my children, my creations. Breathe in

the breath of your creator. Take in his breath and make it your own."

I didn't do drugs, but I had been around enough guys who had to recognize the odor. The breath of the creator smelled an awful lot like marijuana. It must have been some potent stuff if they thought it was going to affect this many people with what felt more like a contact buzz. Now I had an even more urgent reason to find the door. If I didn't get out of here soon, I'd be feeling the affect myself and probably give in to the same urges as everyone else as the drug lowered my inhibitions. Between the visual stimulation being played out before me and the drugs playing with my ability to resist, I didn't stand much of a chance.

Somewhere near the back of the building, I found a curtained room. I'm not even sure how I got there. I thought I was headed to the front. I guess I must have circled around in the crowd instead. Either way, here I was in front of a curtained room with a choice. Go in the room, hoping there will be a back way out, or continue wandering around in a pot smoke filled orgy. Okay, I didn't say it was a great choice, just a choice. I chose the curtain. All I needed now was Monty Hall.

I should have chosen door number two or even the box on the table instead of what I saw behind curtain number one. Back there, on a pedestal, was a large, anatomically correct statue of the creator. Okay, more like anatomically enhanced. He had the same muscular physique, but he also had four sexual organs, and each one of them was being engaged by both men and women. I was going to hurl, big time.

"Hey," a voice said to my left/ the voice came with a large hand that had grabbed my arm. "You can't go into the holy of holies without permission."

"I know that," I stated forcefully. "Everyone knows that. But tell me something. Is the creator in charge?"

"What kind of stupid question is that? Of course he is in charge. He's the creator."

"And as the creator he is powerful?"

"Yes," he said and I could tell I was beginning to confuse him. He was the authority figure here. I was the one in the wrong. I wasn't supposed to be here. But by questioning him, I made it seem as if I were the one in charge.

"So if he's powerful and in charge, I couldn't be here unless it was alright with him. Or are you saying the creator is unable to enforce his rules?"

"No," he stammered, "of course not. The creator can do all."

"I thought so," I said, breaking free of his grip. "Now lead me out of here before I report your blasphemy to the authorities.

"Of course," he said, all too anxious to get rid of

me. He led me to a nearby back emergency door, stuck in his key to disarm the alarm, and opened the door for me. It opened into a dark alleyway.

I was still confused about my whereabouts. I had gone in one door and come out of another on the other side of the building. I should be able to circle around and find Bob's car, but how far had we travelled from Jackee's apartment. Would I be able to find a taxi or would they all be busy celebrating? Oh well, there was only one way to find out. I headed for the other end of the alley and I hoped towards the street we parked on. I'd probably have to walk all the way home, but at least I was out of that place. I had only gone around ten feet when I heard a voice.

"You're in danger," a deep, gravelly voice said. "You have to get out before you lose yourself."

"Isn't that a little hard to do," I replied, "wherever I go, there I am."

"You feel yourself slipping away, don't you? That's why you answer with a smart mouth instead of a smart brain. You have no idea how to handle what is happening to you. There is a way that seems right to a man, but the end thereof is the way of death."

""My way is this way," I answered and pointed in the general direction of the apartment.

"I'm not talking about where you sleep. Soon you will give into your base desires. And when you do, the battle will be lost."

"I already have," I admitted. "Jackee is pregnant with my baby."

"She may be pregnant, and it may be your baby, but you didn't put it there," gravelly voice assured me. He stepped out from behind a dumpster and I saw that he matched his voice. If I had to describe him in one word, I might choose gravelly. He was a big man, but not like the rest of the men I had seen. He was big everywhere. He had a massive barrel chest that only slightly tapered down into his waist. And unlike other men I had encountered, he was fully clothed, from work boots to jeans, a flannel shirt and a long duster.

"What do you mean, my baby, but I didn't put it there? As far as I know, there's only one way for that to happen."

"Forty years ago, that was true, but the times have changed, my friend, and many things have changed with those times, many of them evil. We don't have much time. You must decide now whether you want to know the truth or become comfortable with the lie. Already, you are wavering, aren't you?"

It was true. I was caught between two worlds. I sensed somehow that this man could lead me to the truth. I knew deep in my heart or soul or somewhere that the life I lived today was false. It had a ring of truth to it, but that ring encircled a massive lie. I decided to go with this guy, whoever he was, and try to find out the truth about Jackee, my baby, and the missing year I almost couldn't remember.

"Lead on," I stated. And so he did. I'm not sure how far or how long we walked. Time and distance seemed like faraway concepts when you are in the dark, which I really seemed to be, both literally and mentally. At least down here I was pretty sure I knew which way was up, even if I couldn't tell north from south, or east from west. No matter. Wherever we were going, I seemed to be making progress. As we walked, the tape in my mind began to clear. The newest memories, those which I'm pretty sure were implanted somehow, began to disappear. I don't know if they, whoever they were, used hypnosis, some kind of drug, or some other new means to record over my mind's cassette, but whatever they used seemed to be fading. I said so to my new friend, even though I didn't know his name.

"Those memories will fade completely in a matter of hours," he said. "But if you had stayed much longer, they would have become permanent." Okay, that was just a plum scary thought. I don't like folks messing with my mind. I ain't got much of one to begin with, but what I have is mine. The Army messed with it some, with my permission of course. Although, come to think of it, I don't know if they messed with my mind to get my permission. Part of my job in intelligence analysis was what the Army called PSYOPS, or psychological operations. In order to better understand how it worked, I allowed them to

put me through some deep stuff. I think it was during
that time that I discovered my talent for lucid
dreaming

CHAPTER SIX

He led me behind the dumpster and down into a
manhole. Life was already strange and it seemed to
me like it was determined to become even stranger.
My tour guide strode forth thru the stygian darkness
like he was walking his dog on a sunny afternoon.
Finally, after hearing me slosh through some puddles
and bumping into a wall, he pulled a headlamp from
his pocket and turned it on, illuminating the pathway
in front of him. Now I could see where he was going,
but my own feet still kept tripping over themselves. If
wasn't looking good, but somehow I sensed that it
looked better and brighter the way I was going while
it was dark and murky back the way I came.

It wasn't too late. I could turn back now and still
find my way back. I could find Jackee, take her home,
and raise our baby together. We wouldn't be married,
but we'd have the next best thing. Only the next best
thing didn't seem so great.

I'm not sure how far or how long we walked.
Time and distance seemed like faraway concepts
when you are in the dark, which I really seemed to be,
both literally and mentally. At least down here I was
pretty sure I knew which way was up, even if I
couldn't tell north from south, or east from west. No
matter. Wherever we were going, I seemed to be

making progress. As we walked, the tape in my mind began to clear. The newest memories, those which I'm pretty sure were implanted somehow, began to disappear. I don't know if they, whoever they were, used hypnosis, some kind of drug, or some other new means to record over my mind's cassette, but whatever they used seemed to be fading. I said so to my new friend, even though I didn't know his name.

"Those memories will fade completely in a matter of hours," he said. "But if you had stayed much longer, they would have become permanent." Okay, that was just a plum scary thought. I don't like folks messing with my mind. I ain't got much of one to begin with, but what I have is mine. The Army messed with it some, with my permission of course. Although, come to think of it, I don't know if they messed with my mind to get my permission. Part of my job in intelligence analysis was what the Army called PSYOPS, or psychological operations. In order to better understand how it worked, I allowed them to put me through some deep stuff. I think it was during that time that I discovered my talent for lucid dreaming.

Part of our conditioning was sleep deprivation. They would keep us awake for days, maybe even a week. Time kinda stopped then. We just plodded on, minute my minute. But with a little concentration, I was able to put myself in a dream state, even while I appeared to be wide awake. To be honest, it was the only thing that got me through that stage. I was able to redirect my mind to places I wanted it to go instead of allowing them to take it wherever they wanted. In a sense, even then I was creating my own reality. It's a bit freaky, I know, but it sure did help me deal with their psychological torture. I heard later that some of the same practices they used on us weren't allowed to be used on our prisoners of war. Kinda messed up, ain't it? They can torture us day and night for weeks, to prepare us for what the enemy might do, while at the same time the enemy is enjoying hot meals and warm beds.

I was doing it again. I was diving deep into my own thoughts so I could ignore what was happening around me. The problem is, I can't afford to ignore what's been happening around me. Someone drugged me. I think that's the only way they could implant those memories. There was some talk about drugs guys used in bars to get women to bed. The next day the women wake up with no memory of what happened. That's totally messed up, if you ask me.

"You got a name," I called out to my fearless leader.

"Of course," he answered. And, of course, he didn't volunteer it.

"Wanna share?" I asked.

"Do I have a choice?" It was my turn.

"Of course," I answered. "We have choices every

day."

"But you will bug me until I give in," he guessed. He was one smart cookie. He may not have me totally figured out, but he had that part figured pretty good.

"My name is Blue. Bet you wonder how I ended up with that name."

"No, I do not. My name is Joseph Levisohn. We have about another quarter of a mile to go before I have to blindfold you." Blindfold? I don't think that was part of the deal. I went over everything in my mind and nothing about a blindfold clicked and I told Mr. Levisohn so. "You can turn back," he offered.

Oh yeah. I could turn back. And I could turn left. Then turn right. Then I could put my left foot in, take my left foot out, and shake it all about, because this was a load of hokey pokey. I had no idea where I was. Even in the open, with landmarks to guide me, I often got lost. Hey, some guys have no sense of direction. When it comes to directions, I really have no sense at all. I'm the kind of guy who can get lost in a parking lot. We had taken so many twists and turns that I didn't have a clue how to head back. Mr. Levisohn had me over a barrel and he knew it.

"Just make sure if you use a handkerchief, that you don't blow your nose in it first," I suggested.

"I was actually thinking of wiping the other end," he answered with a smile. Did he actually have a sense of humor? I hadn't thought so until now, but that was definitely a joke, a sick one, but still a joke.

We went that quarter of a mile he spoke of before he turned to me with not a hanky, but a black bag. He was sick. He slipped the bag over my head, spun me around a couple of times, then we took several steps in some direction before I heard something scraping across the concrete and a door opening. We went through the door, I presume, and continued our jolly jaunt into the depths of hell. I could have told Joseph that he could lead me down here without the blindfold, give me a detailed map and a set of instructions, and I still couldn't find my way back. I could have, but I didn't bother. I think I would have ended up wearing the bag anyway. I wanted to ask him if it made my butt look big, but I managed to refrain myself.

Finally, he led me up a flight of stairs, through another door, and into the open air. He removed the bag, but it didn't help much. It had turned dark during the time we had spent in the sewers and maintenance tunnels. I knew that first part was a part of the sewer system, and since the bag didn't cut off my sense of smell, I assumed the second part was a maintenance tunnel. He turned the headlamp back on and led me just a little further to a warehouse. Inside the warehouse was a small office and that's where I finally got to sit down.

"Question?" he asked. Oh yeah, just a few. Like

who the heck are you? Who can I trust here? Can I trust anyone, including you here? Yeah, I had a few questions, but I also knew Joseph was in the lead on this dance, so I stepped carefully.

"We could start with some basic anatomy," I offered. "If my brain ain't completely fried, I figure it's been about a week since I first woke up. If I'm right, how is that Jackee looks about six months pregnant with my baby?"

"That part is easy. You went to the hospital, correct?" I told him that he was right. I had gone through a stream of tests. Stream, it was more like a raging river of tests.

"Yeah, so?" I asked.

"And they took blood, along with other samples, right? Including a semen sample?" Well, that was getting a little personal, but he was right. If I had a fluid in me, on me, or around me, they got a sample of it, including, but not limited to, saliva, sweat, urine, tear drops, blood, and of course the fun one, semen. Some of the nurses, both male and female, offered to help me with that one, but I turned them all down. There just wasn't enough to go around and I was always told that if you don't have enough for all, then keep it to yourself. That's good advice.

"I felt like a doggone pincushion," I admitted. "But what does that have to do with me?"

Joseph took a seat in the big chair behind the desk and folded his hands one over the other. I used to see this same move from Mr. Morris, my wrestling coach/counselor in high school. Back then it meant a lecture was coming, and I was pretty sure it meant the same thing today. Maybe not a "You need to try harder" lecture, but more like a "This is how things are now" lecture.

"Have you ever heard of cloning?" he asked.

"Sure," I answered. "It's real popular in science fiction."

"And it is real popular in science fact," came the reply. "Your so called baby is a clone. Probably a clone of you, although they can mix your genes and her genes for a baby that has two actual parents."

"Whoa! Stop the bus. Are you saying that she managed to get six months pregnant in less than a week.?"

"I'm saying they could have given you a full term baby in a week. It must have served their purpose for you to see the woman pregnant. Probably a bonding thing."

"Her name is Jackee and yeah it worked. I don't care if it is a clone. It's still a baby and it's my baby."

"I understand. I meant no disrespect. We should all respect life, even life born in a test tube, so to speak."

Something was slowly dawning on me. I began to think about Jackee and her perfect body. No, not in that way. Okay, I'm a guy, so in that way too, but it was on the back burner simmering. The other thought was on the front coming to a rolling boil. I thought of not only her perfect body, but of all the perfect bodies. And I began to think about how although each of them were different, they were all also the same. It was like vanilla ice cream. Follow me on this one. You got vanilla, which is great, cause you can just add a little something to it and really jazz it up. But then you got country style, chocolate chip, churn style, and a bunch of other variations on basic vanilla. That was what I was seeing in all of those people. They were all variations of vanilla. It was time to test my theory.

"So Jackee and the others are...." I trailed off my question.

"Not clones, but something similar. They are engineered humans."

"Ain't that the same thing?" I asked, a bit puzzled. Alright, more than a bit puzzled. But this was way past "Double Creature Feature". This was like Frankenstein with the volume pumped up to the max.

"No, not exactly. I'll start at the beginning and give you a summary of events. But please hold your questions to the end." He went from being Mr. Morris to Mrs. Kvetch, my third grade homeroom teacher who did everything she could to live up to her name. Each time she gave a lecture on proper table manners, or not passing gas in class, or some other lame subject, she always started out by telling us to hold our questions, like we were holding our bladder.

"So the Readers Digest version?"

"Yes, exactly. After the great disappearance."

"Whoa, what great disappearance?" I knew I had messed up because his right eyebrow shot up at an improbable angle. Then I realized that he didn't lift his eyebrow. It had taken up permanent residence there. He just tilted his head a little for maximum effect. It worked. I shut up.

"As I was saying, after the great disappearance, a man by the name of Saul Abuajam came forth. The world was already familiar with him as a brilliant scientist, diplomat, and theologian. Well, he was a brilliant theologian until he renounced Christianity, but that's a different story.

Mr. Abuajam claimed that the Christians who were taken were actually aliens who had infiltrated the earth as spies. And, he also claimed that they would be returning to attack the earth soon. So he proposed a solution, bioengineering the human body. His was the first." I know I was risking the wrath of the eyebrow, but I had too many questions and his answers were coming way too slowly for my taste. I figured the disappearance was the rapture, which meant I had missed out on that bus. And I also knew Mr. Abupajamas was right about the return. But they wouldn't be coming back alone. Jesus would be coming back with them and no amount of bioengineering was going to impress him. He was the first to do it with a pile of dirt.

"So what's the difference between bioengineering and cloning?" I asked.

"I was coming to that," he stated firmly. "Mr. Abuajam was the first to demonstrate the process on himself. He used genetic manipulation along with nanobots to recreate his own body. It was a bigger, better body. It was no longer susceptible to disease or aging. According to him, he made himself immortal. He claims that it was how man was always meant to be. According to him, Lucifer was granted by God the ability to make men immortal, but that Jesus, the great enemy, cursed man with aging and disease as punishment for mankind not worshipping him."

"I thought you said he was a brilliant theologian."

"He is. He was able to convince people of his theories using the Bible itself, but you'll see that when you watch his speeches. For now, let me continue."

"Wait a sec," I said. "I think I see where this is going. He claims we all need these bodies, these almost perfect, never gonna die bodies to fight off the big, bad Christians when they return."

"Correct," he said as if praising a student in class.

"But to get the good stuff, you gotta pledge your soul to Lucifer, who has really gotten some bad press and just wants everyone to have fun with sex, drugs, and rock and roll, right?"

"Essentially," he admitted. "Most people went right along with him. They didn't care about fighting Christians when they returned, but almost everyone wanted a new body. Some of those people you see are well over a hundred." I was getting a sick feeling. Was Jackee one of those senior citizens? Was I tempted to make out with a woman who could be my grandma, or even my great grandma? I really needed a place to puke.

"What about you?" I asked. "Why didn't you get a new body?"

"I am a Jew. I don't know much, but I know Satan when I see him. And that man, Saul Abuajam is mixed up with Satan. He claims that it was Lucifer who showed him how to make the nanobots and to manipulate genes."

"I don't doubt that," I said. "Satan would do anything to mess with God, and messing with people is the best way he has to mess with God."

"Agreed," he stated.

"So where do you come down on this?" I asked.

"You believe in Satan, do you believe in Jesus?" He paused a good long while before answering. I let him take all the time he needed. I don't think Joseph was a Christian Jew. If he had been, he would have been taken out with the rapture. But there was always the chance he might become one. That was between him and God. I was just here to answer any questions he might have along the way.

"About Yeshua? I don't know yet. I know he is not the devil. Only the devil is the devil. But I'm not ready to say he Messiah either. As I said, I am a Jew."

"Don't make no difference," I came back. "About being a Jew, I mean. Yeshua was a Jew. So were all the writers of the New Testament. Well, except maybe one. But most of them were. And Jesus taught out of the Old Testament. He used to teach about himself from the law and the prophets."

"Are you trying to convince me, then? Do you think to convert me?" he asked.

"Nope, ain't my job. I just want to point out some truth. You do some research and decide for yourself. But I can almost guarantee that if you look with an open mine, you'll find Jesus all throughout the Old Testament." That was true. I didn't know much about Joseph, except that he seemed to be helping me when he didn't need to. He might have his own agenda, I guess, but until it shows up, I'll do my best to trust him. Besides, it didn't look like I had a whole heck of a lot of choice in the matter. Something he said clicked in my brain. "Did you say something about nanabots?"

"Oh," he said, "so you were listening. Yes, nanobots. Nano is a prefix meaning small or tiny. In this case, microscopic. And then bots, well, I guess you know that refers to robots. So nanobots are teeny, tiny robots injected into the bloodstream. These tiny robots replace the genetic material inside the bodies they are injected into. These new, improved genes then grow and multiply, essentially creating a whole new person. That's why everyone looks to him as creator."

That explained a whole lot, and opened up a whole new can of questions. Some questions were down to earth, like could we fight these things if we needed to? After all, if they didn't suffer from disease, I assumed they had some kind of ability to heal. Could they even be killed? Other questions took more of a "what the heck" kind of form. One of which was, are the even human anymore? And if they were, did they still have souls? They seemed more of Frankenstein monster than human.

"They don't seem to have any kind of a moral compass," Joseph continued. "But I guess you've noticed that already. I don't know if that's a side effect of the gene manipulation or more of a psychological effect."

"Guess that's one for philosophers to ponder," I said. "But I'd go with the psychological thing. Shoot, people in my day did some pretty bad things and they only thought they were going to live forever. Most folks don't need to be taught how to do wrong, it just kinda comes natural to us. We need to be taught how to do right, and even then we mess it up most of the time."

"True," Joseph agreed. "And you are right. It is for better men than you and I to decide the reasons behind their behavior. I am telling you this because I want you to know they won't think twice about killing you. They might think more about running over a squirrel than running over you. Strange ones."

I let that information mull around in my brain for awhile, letting it soak in like gravy soaking into biscuits. Even as a boy I remembered people that cared more for animals than people. It was fine to kill a baby in the womb, but don't you dare fry up a good eagle's egg. Okay, I know you ain't supposed to eat eagles. Even God expects us to take care of our home. Besides, spotted owls taste much better and ain't near as tough to chew.

"The other thing," Joseph continued, "is that they don't age. Many of the people you saw today were alive when you went to sleep. Some of them are much older than you, even with your forty years of sleep."

Alright, that put a sick feeling in my stomach. According to Joseph, I probably hadn't done anything with Jackee except lust after her, which I did with much abandon. No, that's not true. I lusted for her, but it was under control or I would have been jumping her bones the moment I woke up. I wasn't the man I needed to be, especially in this sick world, but I wasn't the man I had been either. My time with the Bible, my time creating my own world and becoming almost godlike in that world, and forty years of sleep and pondering had changed my outlook on life. And now I learned that the rapture had taken place and I was too late for it. That meant I was going to have at least seven years of hell on earth to go through, which bothered me, but not as much as it might have. For one thing, I knew that after seven years or so, I had an eternity up in Heaven. Seven years versus eternity? Yeah, I'd take that trade any day of the week.

And then Jackee came back to my mind. How old was she? Was I lusting after someone's great grandma or worse? Was there anything worse than lusting after a great grandma? Okay, I guess it's alright if you happen to be a great grandpa, but I wasn't. I was barely out of my teens. Well, I was actually sixty and almost ready for social security, but I sure didn't feel like that guy.

"You said that if I had stayed any longer, that I would have been lost. Why do you think that?" I wondered. I wondered a whole lot of things, but that was the biggest one on my mind at the moment. He leaned back in his chair and let his hands rest across his chest before answering.

"It goes back to the nanobots," he started. "They

don't simply disappear after doing their work manipulating your genes. Once inside, they implant themselves in your brain and along your spinal nerves to act as wireless receivers. The government or someone anyway, controls the thoughts of the people this way. In a very real sense, they manipulate time."

"Excuse me?" I said. "A minute is still sixty seconds, isn't it? Aren't there still twenty fours in a day? Or did the nanobots manipulate that somehow?" He chuckled. It was the first real sign of humor I had seen from him. I'm usually pretty upbeat myself, ready to go with the flow and laugh along the way, but somehow none of this seemed funny at all. I was in serious danger of losing my sense of humor, which was totally messed up since I had already lost my sense of direction and was told a long time ago that I never had any common sense. How's a guy supposed to get along in life?

"For you and I, yes, those things are true. Well, it almost wasn't true for you. You lost quite a bit of time, didn't you?" I agreed that I had. A year had gone by in my life without me knowing it, and then again, it hadn't. Man, this was just a little more than confusing.

"So Jackee and everyone else just kind of played along?" I asked.

"No," he stated firmly. "For them a year did pass."

"Huh?" Confusion wasn't the word. This was a mixed up, messed up, total mess. I couldn't tell if I was coming, going, or sitting still and letting everything move around me.

"We don't know how often, maybe every night, maybe once a week, but sometime those in charge download information directly into the brains of those with the nanobots. They also upload memories and store them somewhere."

"They store memories of people? What for? What purpose does it serve?"

"You wouldn't believe the information you gather every day. Most of it is useless, so your brain, like a good computer, puts it in the trash can. Other memories are used for a little bit, then discarded when it's no longer needed."

"Like cramming for a big test and then forgetting everything after the test is over," I suggested.

"One example, but more immediate is you driving down the road. You see something in your field of vision, swerve or brake accordingly, and then move on, forgetting many times what you've just seen."

"Only the computer or whatever it is that is hooked up to these people stores everything and discards nothing, right?"

"Exactly. And in this way it spies on everyone they see without them even knowing it. And the computer or whatever it is happens to be learning."

"Learning? How does a computer learn?"

"The same way you and I do. It learns from experience, from mistakes, from memories. It's called artificial intelligence. This is another gift from Lucifer, I suppose. Men had been working on it for years, but Saul Abuajam had a super computer capable of artificial intelligence in less than a year."

The more I learned, the more I thought that I needed to be back in my little capsule fast asleep. I almost pinched myself to make sure I wasn't there, dreaming all of this. I had watched my share of drive-in sci-fi movies when I was a kid, and read at least a hundred books about the future, space travel, alien invasions, and even mutations caused by radiation, but this was way out of my league. Even Asimov and Heinlein hadn't dreamed up this kind of stuff. This was sci-fi, fantasy, and horror all mixed together with a good dose of Biblical reality. Most people think of the devil as that little dude on the potted meat can with a red suit and pitchfork, but he's real and real dangerous. And it kind of looked like he was running the show for the moment.

I remembered being scared as a kid because there were monsters under my bed or in my closet. Zeke would come in, turn on the lights, inspect the room, including bed and closet, and then proudly proclaim the place to be monster free. He said that there wasn't anything in the dark that wasn't there in the light. That reassured me back then. Between his strong hand and confident walk, I didn't think any monster stood a chance against him. But that was then and this is now. Now the monsters roamed the streets in broad daylight and the scared people scrambled under the beds or hid in the closets. Satan, in one form or another, was roaming the earth.

I know the Bible warned that he was roaming the earth like a roaring lion, seeking whom he could devour. When God talked about Job, Satan said he was going to and fro in the earth and walking up and down in it. But even knowing that, I always had the sense that Satan was on a leash. God would let him do some things, but then yank his chain if he went too far. And whatever Satan did always turned out to be something that God was ready and prepared for. I was sure that God was still in charge, but I had to wonder how long of leash He was letting Satan have at the moment.

"Alright," I said, "two more questions."

"Just two?" Joseph asked.

"For now. I guess two. First, is there a place to sleep around here, cause my teeny tiny little mind needs some time to let all this sink in, and I do that better when I'm asleep."

"Yeah, we have some bedrooms downstairs.

They're not much, but there are beds and blankets."

"Good enough," I answered. "I've slept in foxholes with a dirt mattress and a rock pillow, so a bed and blanket is a night in a luxury hotel."

"Glad to help. So what's the other question?"

"I still don't get the whole time manipulation thing. I mean, a day is a day, isn't it?"

"While you're awake, for the most part. Even then, time can be stretched out if you're waiting on something good, like a pretty date."

"Okay, but even though a minute seems like an hour, it's still a minute. Perceptions change, but reality doesn't change."

"Hmm," he pondered. "True enough, but let me ask you something. How long do your dreams last?"

"They say just a couple of minutes, but it seems like it's longer than that. I could play with time when I was in the capsule. I'd run it back and forth, sometimes living the same day over and over again in my dreams." That's when it hit me. The uploading and downloading of information from the computer was kind of like living in a dream. It could manipulate reality for the people it downloaded to as simply as I manipulated reality in my own dreams. And, according to Joseph, I was in danger of falling into that manipulation, even though I didn't have the nanobots and couldn't receive a direct download. I didn't have any doubts now that if I had stayed with Jackee that I would be volunteering to get a new body within a day or maybe less. And along with the new body would be a bunch of electronic cockroaches infesting my brain and making night day and day into night. The whole prospect was really scary.

"Your other question," Joseph prompted.

"How did this Saul guy get away with it? I mean, wasn't there some resistance to any of it."

"Some, but to understand Saul Abuajam, I think you need to hear him for yourself. We have many of his speeches from his podcasts. Podcasts are kind of like television talk shows that are played on the internet."

"Yeah, I'm familiar with them," I said. I didn't want to look stupid, even though I was still basically ignorant of the world around me, and with each passing moment, my ignorance was being put out their like a shop display in a window on Main Street.

"Of course," he said. "Tomorrow, after a good night's sleep and maybe some breakfast, you can watch his podcasts and get the message straight from the horse's mouth."

Horse's mouth? I was thinking he fit the other end a whole lot better.

CHAPTER SEVEN

Following a night's sleep, not a good night's sleep, just sleep, I asked Joseph about a place to run and maybe a decent workout. I was getting soft in my old age. Besides, a good sweat was just what I needed to clear my mind. He led me to an old gym that had been retrofitted with a few new machines. After a brief lesson on how to use the treadmill and bicycle, he left me alone with my thoughts.

My first thought was about the rapture, or the disappearance of all the Christians. According to Joseph, the first thing to happen was the gathering and ultimate imprisonment of everyone who even thought about being a Christian. They were sent to detainment facilities for reconditioning and sensitivity training. Those who were willing to renounce their beliefs were allowed to rejoin society on a probationary basis. About half of those who were taken into the detainment camps renounced their faith in Jesus within a year, most of those within the first month. That was disappointing, but not really all that surprising. There were a lot of people he remembered from his youth who were Christian in name only. Some of them went to church because it was the "right" thing to do. Others went because their parents had gone and it was more or less tradition. And there were still others who went for social or business gains. It was sad, but true.

The first incarcerations began about three years

ago. But they weren't isolated to the United States. It was a worldwide phenomenon. In fact, it started in Europe, and then quickly spread to Asia, Africa, The Middle East, and then the rest of the world, including the United States, who was the last to start the round up. At least I had that much to hold on to. We held on to the last before collapsing into fascism and tossing our liberties and legacy down the toilet.

About two years after the first prisoners were rounded up, most of them disappeared, along with several thousand more who had either never been caught or who had deceived their captors by falsely renouncing their faith. I sorta wondered how things went for them when they stood face to face with Jesus. It's not for me to judge, but let's just say I wouldn't want to be them. Of course, then again, at this point, I'd rather be them than me.

The sweat was pouring off me, my heart was racing, and my muscles were aching, but my head refused to clear. I think part of the problem was that I was running on a treadmill with a fan in my face under the glare of fluorescent lights instead of being outside with the wind in my face under the glare of the morning sun. Some things just couldn't be reproduced or imitated, like banana flavoring. A banana is a banana and a run up and down hills is, well, you get the picture.

The problem was that I just couldn't wrap my head around all that had happened while I was in la-la land. I guess what really bothered me was just a matter of timing. If I had gotten saved just a little earlier in my deep sleep, I would have woken up in Heaven instead of what looked like it was going to be hell on earth. What can I say, I'm just lucky that way.

I was on my third set of twenty push-ups when it hit me like a ton of bricks. I was lucky that way. Other people got to hear about history and wonder about where their place in it was. I had mine handed to me on a silver platter. Yeah, that thing I said earlier about swapping places with some of those who got to go in the rapture, scratch that. I was exactly where and when I needed to be. It definitely was gonna suck for awhile, but that's life after all, ain't it. Life is good, life is bad, then it gets worse for awhile, and after a little bit, it just downright sucks eggs. This was no doubt the suck egg part of the situation. Or was it? Life wasn't too hard yet.

It was then that I came up with my theorem. It wasn't a hard set law like Murphy had, but for me it was a stroke of genius. Well, if not a stroke, at least a small mark. You know how people always say that they wished that they had been born in another time. Some people think they would have been great cowboys, while others want to be the white knight charging in on his faithful steed to slay the dragon, or whatever foe was on deck for the week, and rescue the fair maiden. We all talk like that some point in our lives, but I've come to a conclusion about these people. There is a name for the malady that possesses them

And that was the other thing that bothered me. Okay, don't get me wrong, I wasn't looking forward to sucking eggs. No one does. But why wasn't I an egg sucking dog right now? I was under the impression that the rapture of the church signaled the beginning of the end. You know, the Christians disappear, the world is in chaos, it totally stinks to be on the earth, whether or not you get saved after the rapture, Satan and the Anti-Christ rule for a bit, and then the whole thing wraps up with Jesus riding in to save the day. The only problem was, I wasn't hearing the clock ticking. There was no doomsday clock counting down from seven years to eternity, so to speak. That meant that the tribulation period might not start for awhile, and meantime, I'm here basically twiddling my thumbs. I didn't know what else to do.

Of course, any good battle plan begins with intel and I knew just where to get that. Joseph said that all of Saul Abupajamas had a bunch of podcasts to view on the internet. Podcasts. What a stupid concept. First of all, pods are for beans or peas, and, of course, for alien races that come here to take over the world. I was kinda assuming that Saul fit into that last category. Just from my brief encounter with him the other night and from what Joseph said, this guy sounded like he was more than one bubble off of plumb. He wasn't just one banana short of a bunch, he was a bunch short of a bunch, like someone had eaten all the bananas and just left the skins hanging on the tree.

I showered and put on the clothes Joseph provided, a tight pair of jeans and a t-shirt with the picture of the ugliest cat I had ever seen. Seriously, this thing looked like it was sucking on an unripe persimmon while it had a lemon up its butt. Jackee had shown me videos of this stupid cat on stupid podcasts and just cracked up with hilarity. I didn't get it. What's so stinking funny about an ugly cat? And does no one here really have anything better to do than follow their ignorant pets around hoping they do something cute? She said that cat had millions of hits, and I believed her, cuz I wanted really bad to hit whoever posted the video to begin with. I had more important videos to watch, but as it turned out, watching cat videos might have been a little more entertaining.

I shared with her some jokes we used to tell about a hundred things to do with a flat cat, like use them for ping-pong paddles or to signal traffic or as fans on hot days. She didn't think my jokes were funny and I didn't think her videos were funny, but at least I didn't run from the room crying. Guess Dylan was right and the times really are a changin'.

Joseph helped me connect to the internet and directed me to the website where Saul's podcasts were backlogged. Turns out he had millions of hits as well and as it turned out, by the time I had watched the first video, I wanted to hit him too. Maybe that crazy doctor was right and I had some anger issues, but I don't thinks so. Stupid people doing stupid things and putting them out in public for other stupid people should make anyone angry and the one with the issues is the one who can't keep his private life private.

I started with the first podcast video.

"Hello, my brothers," Saul said as he looked into the camera with a friendly smile. He was young. I'm guessing he was just a little older than me, maybe a year or two, but no more. He had black wavy hair, green eyes, a dark, flawless complexion and a warm, friendly smile. That last part was totally deceitful.

"My name is Saul Abuajam. As most of you know, I was born in Jerusalem to parents of both Jewish and Muslim descent. I am the child of a Middle Eastern Romeo and Juliet, although my story, in many ways is even more of a tragedy than those star crossed lovers.

My mother is Jewish. Through genetic testing and extensive research, we have been able to trace her lineage back through the line of David, She is not a direct descendant of David, as I had hoped, but we believe she, and consequently I, are direct descendants of his sister, Abigail, who bore the children of Jether the Ishmaelite.

My father, on the other hand is a Muslim. And we have traced his roots as far back as my mother's. This was also done through genetic testing and much research. The results were very interesting, if not downright startling. My patriarchal lineage traces back to this same Jether the Ishmaelite, who was the father of Amasa, the captain of the host of the armies of Israel under Absalom, son of David.

Why do I share all of this with you? This will come clear in due time. For now, let it suffice to say that I can speak with authority to both worlds. Worlds which have been separated for generations by the forces of evil. Worlds which will once again be reunited by love, as it was with Jether and Abigail, instead of divided by hate as it is today."

Okay, so far, so good. I don't know how he went from this kind of geeky looking genealogist to what looked like the leader of most of the world, but I had to admit, he had a point, anytime love conquered hate was a good thing. Or that's what most people always thought.

I went into my deep sleep during the Iranian hostage crisis. A lot of people just wanted to turn Iran into a big glass parking lot with a couple of well placed nukes. It wasn't very practical, I'll admit, but it showed the frustration everyone was feeling over the situation. After all, we were a stinking super power, for pities sake. And they were holding our people like a bunch of common street thugs. I didn't understand the politics of it all, and still don't. Don't think most people do. I don't think the people who did the kidnapping or the people who were kidnapped understood it all either. It was just a part of the times we lived in.

I watched some more of the podcasts.

"My brothers and sisters, both of Jews and Moslems, I appeal to you today as few people can. You know my history. You know who I am and what I have done. You know the shame I lived with for years after being rejected by both my mother's people and my father's people. I was an outcast. I was a stranger in a strange land. I was a man without a country. I was a man without a heritage, although my heritage on both sides of my family was rich, Still, I was poor.

For our safety, my father decided to move our family to the United States, where he could raise his family in peace and seek for prosperity. He wanted to give our family a chance to not only survive, but to thrive.

And it was there, in that land of great evil, that God chose to reveal himself to me in unexpected ways. It was there that my family realized I was different from others. I was a genius.

I do not say this with boasting. Allah granted me this gift, although I would not admit it at the time. Allah forgive me.

Because I was rejected by both religions, I chose to reject both religions. In fact, I turned against God himself. If he did not want me, then I did not want him.

I sought a new god, one that would bring me the answers I craved, one that would grant me peace in my heart and in my soul, one that would explain to me the mysteries of who I was and where I came from. My new god was science and I laid myself bare on that altar.

I graduated from MIT with a bachelor's degree in mathematics at the age of thirteen. Four years later, I graduated from the same institution with a doctorate in Physics. I do not tell you these things as boasting, but rather to let you know that I did indeed offer myself to this new god."

I gotta admit, I was impressed. There were a lot of kids I went to school with who couldn't read the diploma they were handed after graduating from high school. Some of them couldn't spell MIT, much less graduate from there. I wasn't smart enough to scrub the toilets in a place like that, and this guy had graduated from there not once, but twice. Okay, so he was one smart cookie, no doubt about that. But how did he go from point A to point B. Point A being just another child prodigy genius who burned himself out by the age of thirty and point B being the guru who persuaded most of the world to reject Jesus and embrace a new religion of self indulgence. Okay, so that last one wasn't really that hard. Most people, given half the chance, would indulge their own fantasies if it wasn't for the so called "norms" of society. But if you could change what was acceptable in people's mind, then you could change society. Shoot, you could set everything on its head, which is what he had done.

This guy had started out life pretty rough, the same as I had. He had parents that loved him, but the rest of his family had rejected not only him, but his whole family, forcing them to flee to a new life. Of course, if it hadn't been for that new life, they might not have discovered his talents, nor had the opportunity to take advantage of those talents. Besides, so what if he had it rough. Lots of people had a rough start in life. It shouldn't be an excuse for screwing up your life or the rest of the world for that matter. We get what we get in life and it's up to each of us to do the best with what we get.

I decided to listen to more of his ranting. Maybe I'd pick up a clue or two on how to handle this guy if it ever came to that. I'd have to admit that if it came to a battle of wits, I was carrying a pocket knife and he had a whole nuclear arsenal. And he looked more than a match for me physically. Of course, I wouldn't let that stop me from trying if it came to that. What he had in brains and muscle, I could make up for with sheer insanity and a massive amount of stubbornness. I didn't suffer from insanity, I enjoyed every minute of it.

"In time, though, I realized that science was a

false god."

Well score one for the brainiac. He had taken years to figure out what most of us seemed to know by instinct, but at least he had figured it out.

"So I began a search for someone who was worthy of my worship, and I thought I had found him. I looked to the one who hung on a cross for my sins. I thought that perhaps in him I could find the one who might fill the emptiness in my soul.

I gave myself to this pursuit with the same abandon that I had given to the false god of science. I researched each of the major Christian denominations, weighing each of them in the balance until I could find the one that best exemplified the teachings of Jesus the Christ. In the end, I settled up Catholicism. I found that the balance between good works, faith, grace, and rituals best suited my needs. Other denominations had good points and bad points. Even Catholicism had some detriments, but I decided at the time that they were insignificant when compared with the overall teachings of Jesus.

I moved quickly up the hierarchal ladder of the Catholic Church. Having never been married, I was welcomed into the priesthood. My eagerness, along with my intelligence, moved me quickly higher and higher, until I had the ear of the Pope himself. I imagine that my notoriety also figured into this quick escalation. Since I was a prominent scientist with several patents and quite a large fortune, the

Cardinals, along with others in power thought to best use me by placing me in proximity to the Pope.

It was there, in the Vatican, that I began to do my best research. I was privy to secrets that had been hidden from the eyes of the public for thousands of years. Some of it was inconsequential, but there were stories of harassment and persecution against Jews, Moslems, and even other Christians. Some of this I knew already, and although I did not agree with, I saw it as history best forgiven and forgotten. But there are some things that cannot be either forgiven or forgotten, at least not by people of good conscience."

He went on, and on, and on about the horrible things done to people of other faiths for years upon years. I knew some of it. I knew something about the Crusades. Okay not much and most of it I probably learned from movies that weren't historically accurate, but I did know a little. I also knew a little about the Inquisition. Again, very little and most of it from poor sources, but even then I knew that there was a lot of bad stuff done to other people in the name of Jesus. I also knew that when Jesus came back and settled scores, there were gonna be a lot of people who he wasn't gonna be happy with. And I didn't figure they would be all that happy with his decisions, but there's only one judge that really counts in the end and he wears a white robe, not a black one.

So the Catholics weren't exactly coming up roses in this guys mind. I guessed it was time for him to

switch religions again. And I wasn't disappointed.
Where he went, though, really took me for a loop. I
should have seen it coming, but I had missed about
forty years of history and was just now starting to
come up to speed. That's another thing about watching
stupid cat videos, it warps your brain and probably
causes some form of brain damage that can't be fixed
with modern medicine.

"My brothers and sisters, both of the Jews and the
Moslems, I ask you something so simple and yet so
profound that even our wisest sages have missed it for
generations. I ask you this: who is it that benefits from
Jews and Moslems hating one another? Is it not the
church, both Catholic and Protestant, which savages
our lands and rapes our people? Do they not profit
from our oil and other commodities? Do they not
profit from selling weapons and arms to both sides of
the conflict?

Have we forgotten our history? Was there not a
time when Jews and Moslems shared the land in
peace? Have we forgotten that we are indeed family?
My ancestors, Isaac and Ishmael shared one father,
Abraham. And it was to our one father that the
promise of blessing was given. It was promised that
all of the world would be blessed through Father
Abraham and his descendants. And has not the world
been blessed indeed by both sides of the family?

And who corrupted these great religions but that
interloper Jesus Christ, who at one time said he came

to bring peace, but also claimed to bring a sword. He said he came to bring forgiveness, but then spoke of severe judgment. He said he came to set us all free, but then the church he founded brings a multitude of rules and regulations to the world, forcing them to conform to their image in order to have peace with God. Are these things not so?

But our people, both our peoples, have lived together in peace and may do so again when this scourge of Christianity has been dealt with and eradicated. We must unite, my brethren, to face this great threat against our people. Does not the Psalmist say that it is good and pleasant when the brethren dwell together in unity? And does not the same Psalm compare this to the oil running down Aaron's beard, a symbol of God's presence and blessing?"

Whew, I had seen people twist the Bible before but this guy was a spiritual contortionist. He handled the Bible like a big piece of saltwater taffy, first twisting it one way to say one thing, and then twisting it again to have it say something else. Joseph was right about one thing, this bozo was some kind of theologian. Only people with a higher education can take something so simple and mess it up so badly. But he was just getting started. He said much more about how the poor people had been persecuted, tortured, raped, and murdered by the rest of the world. And, of course, by the rest of the world, he meant Christians. He finally came around to saying so near the end of this round of ranting. He excused the rest of the religions, including pagans and even those who worshipped Satan by saying that they were pawns of the real rulers of this evil world, the Christians. But what he had to say next really blew my socks off.

"Welcome my brethren. And now I extend that welcome to all peoples who are not Christians. For do we not in essence serve the same God? Do not all roads eventually lead to the same place? Do not all of us seek that which is above us?

And tell me, my brothers and sisters, is not God infinite? Does he not fill all of eternity? And if he does, is it not possible and plausible that he appears to all of us according to our cultures and needs? Does he not appear to each of us in different forms? And why not if He is indeed an infinite God? Why should such a god limit himself to one form and seclude himself to one people? And yet this is exactly what the Christians would have you to believe. They would have you to believe that there is only one road to heaven, their road. They would have you believe that there is only one door that opens to God's love and power, their door. They would have you believe that there is only one way to reach the highest of all, their way.

And why do they teach such things? I have the answer for you, but prepare to be shocked. This answer is surprising, but not if you have studied the words and teachings of this false god, Jesus, as I have for years.

The answer to their arrogance is simple. They are
not of this world, as their savior is not of this world.
He said as much when he came here from his world,
wherever that was. He told his disciples that his
kingdom was not of this world. What could this mean
except that he was an alien who had taken human
form? Was his birth not by means other than normal?
Do we not have stories even today of women taken
into spaceships and implanted with hybrid humans?
He told Pilate, the governor who recognized that he
was an alien, that Pilate could have no power over
him unless it was granted from above. Is this not an
admission of being an alien? Do not their scriptures
teach that they are aliens and pilgrims on this planet?

They multiply by means of an alien symbiosis.
One infected with a symbiot reaches out to other
humans in order to multiply their kind. I believe that
the symbiot cannot be passed on to unwilling hosts.
They must be welcomed in to your body freely. This
is our salvation. If we reject the teachings of this alien
messiah and his disciples, then we may yet save our
planet. Our only hope is to incarcerate all of those
who claim to be Christians. Allow those then who are
incarcerated a chance to reject their alien symbiosis.

Once captured, they are still dangerous. We must
be careful and on our guard. There are stories
throughout history of those who have been captured
ensnaring their guards with this alien presence. We
cannot be too careful in this matter. We must begin
segregating this alien race from our women and

children while there is a chance."

Wow! This nut was totally "Twilight Zone". I expected Rod Serling to step into the camera at any moment, or at least Forrest Whitaker. There were several other things he said, but by now I think we all get the gist of what his theory was and anything else he added to it wouldn't be much. For instance, he claimed that all of the healings that Jesus did were done by the alien symbiotes Furthermore, he claimed that the High Priest, along with Pharisees and Sadducees recognized that he was an alien and that he performed the miracles he did using that alien power. They said that he cast out demons and performed his deeds by Baal-Zebub, which, according to Saul, really meant Lord of the flying ones.

To say that was a stretch was like saying the Grand Canyon was just a big hole. But the strange thing is that people ate it up like it was a steak dinner with all the trimmings and they hadn't eaten for days. I knew that because intermixed into his podcast were news highlights, most of them showing the Christians being rounded up, others highlighting interviews with some "former" Christians, most of them predominant mainstream pastors of mega-churches, who suddenly had an epiphany and were now preaching the gospel according to Saul. Some of their churches were converted into makeshift compounds which then became internment camps. Most of the guards at those camps were former deacons and other staff members from those churches.

The one thing that really caught my attention was an item about John the Baptist, who, according to Saul, came to gather intelligence and analysis for the coming invasion. Saul said that John was beheaded because King Herod had listened to his lovely wife Herodias, who had been given special insight by God in a dream. She told him that the alien symbiotes took control of the hosts mind. That's why the alien messiah told his disciples to love him with all their heart, soul, and mind. Later this was confirmed by others in the resistance, which is what true Jews were called supposedly, when Paul told his followers that they were not to be conformed to this "world", but be transformed by the renewing of the mind. So, she told Herod that in order to truly kill an alien, you must remove its head.

That hit me right between the eyes. I was pretty doggone sure that during the tribulation period people get separated from their heads on a fairly regular basis. I wasn't afraid to die when God was through with me. In fact, I was kinda looking forward to getting out of Dodge in a hurry, but I also felt like I had some unfinished business to take care of before I caught that bus. Guess I was feeling a little bit like Paul when he said he couldn't make up his mind about dying. Like me, he was ready to go home, but also like me, he had some stuff to handle before he did. Oh well, it wasn't my call to make anyway, so I might as well just enjoy the ride as much as I could until God decided it was time for me to come home. I had just eased back in my seat, closed my eyes, and began a short prayer when I heard her voice for the first time.

"Hello," she said, "my name is Tye Chee. What's yours?"

The office was quiet and dark, and to be honest, just a little spooky. So when she interrupted my prayer, I about hit the ceiling. In fact, there are indentations up there now that weren't there before. I'm not saying I made them, but they match my finger pattern. When I finally caught by breath and did a little meditative CPR to get my heart pumping again, I looked for the source of my fright.

She was absolutely stunning. I'm not one to assign ages to people, especially since Joseph told me that some of the hot women I saw in town were old enough to be my great grandmothers, but I would guess she was in her late teens, maybe early twenties. She was gorgeous. Or did I mention that already. She had shoulder length light brown hair, green eyes, a cute aquiline nose and a full, rich mouth that curved just so.

She was lean and tall, but not bony or wiry. There was definitely some flesh there, and it was just where it needed to be. Her breasts were small, but full and looked firm. Her stomach was flat, but her hips were full and round. Did I mention she was beautiful? Because she was absolutely breathtaking.

But the most striking thing about her appearance was her flaws. I know that sounds a little weird, but it's true. Her complexion wasn't flawless. There were shadings in her skin tone. One arm was a little darker than the other, something I used to see in those who drove military convoys. Her face had some lines, just little ones that were precursors of what would be character lines when she was a great deal older. There were even some pock marks from former pimples and if I wasn't mistaken, she still had a couple of pimples. Gorgeous!

I was in love.

"Hello," she said again. "I'll say it slower so maybe you can understand. My name is Tye Chee. What's your name?" She spoke slower, as if she were on an old movie, talking like an explorer to a native in a foreign land. I never understood how saying the same thing, only slower, was supposed to make it easier to understand. But it must have worked, though, because I finally spoke up.

"My name is Blue. And I think I'm meant to marry you someday."

CHAPTER EIGHT

I wasn't exactly sure how she was going to take that, but I was more than a little surprised by her response.

"I think I could live with that," she said nonchalantly. "But you'll have to get it by my Uncle Joseph."

So this was Joseph's niece? It's not that I didn't think he didn't have family. I guess in the rush of rescue and the need for me to gather information, I just never thought about whom else might be here. But her presence made me think about the rest of the people who might be in the neighborhood. To be honest, her presence made me think about a lot of other things, but I had to keep them under control for the moment; out of sight and out of mind. Yeah, right. Who was I trying to kid? Not myself, since I'm pretty sure it was my body having those feelings and my brain having those thoughts. The funny thing is, I wasn't thinking with my lower extremities, as I had done in the recent history. Jackee also brought out feelings and desires. But those desires were on a baser, more instinctual level. With her, I was a cat on the prowl, waiting patiently to strike and make my kill. I was an animal on the prowl and she was to be a victim of my insatiable appetite.

Wow! I didn't even know I could think like that, much less self analyze. Who needs fancy offices, couches, and men with a pencil and a notepad when all you have to do is think for yourself. I guess it wasn't as easy as all that or I'd do a whole lot more of it and maybe keep myself out of a little more danger and a lot more bad situations.

With Tye Chee, I immediately wanted to get to know her. I wanted to talk to her, find out her feelings on different things, and find out what her favorite foods were and how she liked her eggs cooked in the morning. I needed to know that because I was already thinking about fixing her breakfast in bed the day after our wedding and for every anniversary after that until I was too old to safely leave in the kitchen alone.

"What kind name is Tye Chee?" I asked, just a little more than curious.

"What kind of name is Blue?" she responded defensively. I guess I struck a nerve. Sometimes it's not what you say or even how you say it, but who you say it to. I had the feeling that this wasn't the first rodeo for her concerning her name. She had ridden that bronco more than once and had gotten thrown several times early on before taming it.

"Sorry," I apologized. "I didn't mean anything by it. I was just wondering where it came from. It's kinda pretty. I like unique names. Makes a body seem a bit more interesting. My name is Blue cuz the folks that found me said I had a jumper on with a little blue horn on it. Said it reminded them of little boy blue. So they just called me Blue for short." I was rambling, and to make things worse, I knew I was rambling and I was powerless to stop it. She had a strange effect on me. I wanted to tell her my life's story, as short and as boring as it was.

"Cool," she said. "Alright, you shared with me, so I'll share with you. My mom and dad were Christians who got rounded up when I was seventeen. That was about three years ago, so I'm twenty if you're wondering." I was wondering. And I was glad that she volunteered the information.

"I'm sorry to hear that," I said and I meant it. Too many people had taken too many children away from their parents, away from people who loved them and cared for them.

"Thanks. Anyway, we were living in Tyronza, Arkansas. It's a little one horse town just northeast of Memphis, Tennessee. Do you know where Memphis is?"

"Yeah, as a matter of fact, I grew up about three hours from Memphis. Don't think I ever made it to Tyronza, but I'd heard of it. Nice town from what I hear."

"I guess. Better than some, worse than others."

I liked her attitude. She was right. Towns are just towns. And, like most things, they can either be better or worse than they are and there are always things better by comparison and worse by the same comparison.

"Okay, so that explains the Tye. How's that spelled anyway?"

"Just like it sounds, I guess. T-Y-E. The E is silent, but I hardly ever am." I could see that. And I could learn to like that. Who was I trying to kid? I already liked that a lot, along with several other things about her. Her honest approach to things was just one of them.

"So where does the Chee come from? Friend of the family or some other town or nearby. Or maybe it's one y'all passed through some time or another."

"Do you always do that?" she asked.

"Do what?" I wondered.

"Talk without thinking about what you're saying. It's kind of cute, in a nerdy sort of way, but I can see where it could get you in a bit of trouble." I was talking way too much. It's one of the things I do when I'm nervous, especially when I'm nervous because I'm around a woman. Make that a beautiful woman and I'm pretty much a blithering idiot. I had to work hard to regain control of myself.

"Sorry," I said. "So where does the Chee in Tye Chee come from? I like the way it sounds."

"Thanks," she responded. "Me too. I've become attached to it over the years. But I'm not real happy sharing where it came from. It's kind of silly and you'll probably laugh and I'll probably have to hit you and then you'll probably never talk to me again."

"No, I promise." I stated.

"You won't laugh," she said, hopefully.

"No, you won't hit me. You might try, but I'll block it or dodge it. Then you'll probably get mad and try even harder, but by then you'll be frustrated and lose control, which will make it even easier for me. That will get you even more frustrated, so you'll try again, miss again, and by this time you'll realize its hopeless, give up and just laugh at yourself. So let's cut to the part where you tell me where your name came from, we'll both have a good laugh, and then go get some lunch because I'm starving."

"Feeling pretty cocky, aren't you?"

"No, just confident. So where did the Chee come from?"

"Fine. But no laughing. My mom had morning sickness almost the whole time she was carrying me and the only thing she could keep down consistently were Cheetos. Happy?"

I didn't laugh. It was hard. No, hard isn't the word for it. It was a monumental task worthy of Hercules or Samson. It took that kind of strength. But I was determined not to hurt her feelings and I could tell this was a sensitive subject for her. Besides, I had grown up fighting half of my life because of being named Blue. The only thing I could think of that might be worse would be to be the title character in that old Johnny Cash song. A boy called Blue might get you several fights in elementary school, but by the time I reached Junior High and especially High School, I had more important things to fight about, like my lack of family heritage and people who knew my story and decided that Zeke and Miss Martha were fair game. I proved to several people that some things and some people were off limits.

"I like it," I finally declared after holding my breath long enough to make a Navy Seal proud. "It has character." Then I added, "Like you."

She was actually taken off guard for just a moment. It was a momentary slippage of her defenses, but hopefully it was all that I needed. I thought about this morning, running in place. I don't know who invented the treadmill, and I won't put him in the same category as the guy who does cat videos, but there's something lacking in running in place. It's like eating diet food. It fills up your stomach, but it doesn't satisfy your real desire for taste, so naturally you find more to eat. In the end, you were better off just eating what you wanted to begin with, just less of it.

The treadmill felt the same way. Sure, I got some exercise, but it didn't satisfy my need to hit the open road. Maybe Tye Chee could help with that.

"How about a walk?" I asked. "Or better yet, maybe there's a couple of ten speeds around."

"Ten speeds?" she asked incredulously. "What century are you from?" It was then that a light went on in her eyes. "You're him, aren't you?"

"I'm a him, but I don't know if him him. Which him are you looking for?"

"The sleeper. Rip Van Winkle from the eighties. Oh this is so cool. We're studying the eighties in one of my college classed. Go on, say something."

"Something," I responded, not knowing what she was hoping for me to say.

"No, no," she corrected. "Say something eighties. Like a catch phrase or a movie line or even some song lyrics if you can sing."

I was beginning to get annoyed. I liked her and all, but to be thought of as a living museum piece was just a little much for me to put up with. For one thing, it put me in the category of old fogey. I may have actually been sixty years old, but I was still physically twenty years old. Okay, maybe twenty and a half. They did think I would age a little while asleep, just not much.. Half a year for every forty or so, yeah, that was the kind of swap I could live with.

The other thing was that I slept through the eighties. And if the videos I watched at Jackee's were any indication, then good riddance. I didn't know anything about the eighties and I told her so.

"You got the right guy, but the wrong decade," I said. "I went to sleep in the beginning of nineteen eighty. I know Ronald Reagan was the president, which blew my mind, but not much else. Sorry." She was disappointed, I could tell. Her jaw dropped a little, and her eyes lost a bit of sparkle, but she wasn't going to let it ruin the moment.

"Fine, "she said. "Then say something from the seventies. Same criteria, different decade."

"Hmm," I stalled. I wasn't sure what she wanted to hear. She seemed as fixated on shallow stuff like movies and music as Jackee was. It seemed like all everyone cared about anymore was the fluff. I mean, millions of people were arrested, incarcerated in prison camps, and then mysteriously vanished, and all people wanted to talk about was the latest video trending on the internet or the latest celebrity gossip to come across the wire. In all the time I spent with Jackee, I never figured out what a Kardashian was or why I would want to keep up with it. But if Tye wanted fluff, I'd give her fluff.

"Live long and prosper," I said, holding my hand in a "V" shape with two fingers as either leg of the "V" and the thumb extended out. Any self respecting Vulcan would be proud of my effort, but Tye wasn't.

"Come on, I said seventies, not modern day. There were several of those movies made during my lifetime." Wow, tough crowd. Guess I'd have to try a little harder. So I gave her my best "Rocky".

"Adrian, Adrian," I cried.

"Oh, please, they must have made a dozen of those by now." She was wrong. I checked and they only made about a half dozen. Still, I wasn't impressing her much.

"Alright, try this one," I said. I put out my hand and opened the fingers in the same "V" as earlier, only this time my hand was flat and extended. I told her to do the same thing to her hand and put her fingers in with mine at a ninety degree angle. It took some coaxing and a little more explanation, but she finally got it.

"Like this?" she asked.

"Yeah, that's it," I said. "Na-noo, na-noo," I said.

"Cool," she said. "Is this some kind of foreplay?'

"No," I said and snapped my hand back. "It's from a television show."

"Is that all you got?" she asked. Once again, my irritation meter was pegging out to its limits. I didn't pay all that much attention to what was going on around me. I never realized there would be a pop quiz forty years later.

"I could tell you fat mama jokes," I offered.

"I don't even know my mother, and you want to insult her? How does that make sense?"

"It was the seventies," I countered. "We didn't have to make sense."

"Well, try again."

"You wanna know what I'm going to do? Just for

the heck of it?"

"What's that?" she asked.

"I'm going to take my right foot, and I'm going to whop you on that side of the face. And you wanna know something? There's not a darn thing you're gonna be able to do about it."

"I'd like to see you try," she said, getting into a defensive posture.

"Sorry," I said. "It was a movie quote from the early seventies."

"It wasn't very nice."

"Neither were the seventies. War protests were still going on. We had a President lie to our faces. People spit on soldiers who were just trying to do their jobs. Women were out burning their bras to prove they didn't need men, which never made a bit of sense to me. We had nuclear holocaust hanging over our heads, along with the threat of cold war."

"Doesn't sound too different from right now," she said.

"Guess not," I agreed. "Solomon was right. What goes around comes around."

"Solomon said that?" she asked.

"He said it nicer, but it's the same basic message.

Hey, got one more for you. Up your nose with a rubber hose."

"That's not very nice, either. I don't want to do this anymore. Let's do something else." That was the opening I was looking for.

"How about a walk?" I suggested. She hesitated a little, but then gave in to my suggestion. We couldn't walk out in the open like I would have preferred, but there were some alleyways and back areas that weren't monitored and she led me down them.

While we walked, I asked her about the secrecy and my rescue from what a lot of men would call paradise. It reminded me of that Monty Python movie where a man is rescued from a castle full of beautiful women. In some ways it felt like my rescue was more of a kidnapping, but I knew better. If I had stayed just a little longer it would have meant my virtual imprisonment with Jackee. Who knows, maybe once I was really hooked, she might have kicked me to the curb and left me to fend for myself, which couldn't have been too hard since I didn't see anyone there working. I guess the government, such as it was, found ways to feed people. Maybe those nearly perfect bodies don't need much nourishment. Either way, I was glad to be rescued, kidnapped, whatever.

I remembered the legend of the lotus eaters and told it to Tye. She had never heard of it before and I probably got a lot of the details wrong. I learned about it in Literature class back in the seventh grade, but I also learned about Loretta Van Dyne in seventh grade and she was a lot more interesting than Literature. But mythology was pretty interesting also, so I paid a little more attention to that than to Dickens or especially the poets.

Tye agreed that those in the city had a lot in common with the lotus eaters. They were too stupefied to realize they were just dead men walking. They had all of the freedom anyone could ask for and still they were imprisoned in their own desires and lusts. It was kind of a strange paradox.

"And what about you?" I asked.

"What do you mean?" she wanted to know. I had been wondering how to approach this subject and this seemed like as good as an opportunity as I was likely to get.

"You said your parents were taken, but here you are, so I know you weren't a believer then, but how about now. What do you think of Jesus?" It was a pretty straight forward question and I was hoping for a straight forward answer. If I understood things right, then we weren't in the actual tribulation period, but I knew it couldn't be far away. Or at least I assumed it couldn't be. I really thought the rapture would be the trigger for everything, the match that lit the fuse, but here we were in a kind of dramatic pause before the big show. If it wasn't the rapture, then the next big thing to happen would be the signing of a peace treaty between the Jews in Israel and the rest of the Muslim world. With Saul preaching a kind of sibling love fest, that couldn't be too far away. I had checked with Joseph earlier and he assured me no such treaty existed, but he also thought it would come soon.

"I'm just not sure. My professors in college make him out to be some kind of monster, but I know mom and dad weren't aliens or anything like that. They were good people who tried to raise me right and do good things for other people. I just wish I knew what the truth was."

"That might be part of your problem," I suggested. "The truth isn't a what, but a who."

"Huh," she said and furrowed her brow in a way that was so cute that I almost lost my train of thought. Her nose crinkled and her lips formed into a perfect pout.

"Jesus is the truth. He said so himself. He said he was the way, the truth, and the life. Nobody comes to the Father except through him. It's really pretty simple. We owe God a debt."

"Why do I owe God anything?" she demanded.

"Because you've sinned, or done wrong. We all have and because of that God has to punish us, but he doesn't want to."

"Okay, I get that," she said. "Everyone does wrong, some more than others I guess, but we all mess up."

"Exactly," I agreed. "But Jesus came here to take our punishment so we don't have to. He's the only one who lived a perfect life, and he makes a trade with us if we ask him."

"I remember mom and dad saying something about that. I wish I had paid more attention, but I was kind of rebellious. And then they were gone, and everyone said Jesus took them. I was so mad and I just couldn't stand to hear anything about Jesus, but I've calmed down since then and I'm able to look at it differently."

I stepped up a short retaining wall to walk on the grass on the other side. It was good to feel real grass and real dirt under my feet. I didn't hate the feel of concrete the way some raised in the country do, but I much preferred real earth when I could get it. I reached down my hand and helped Tye up. After that I didn't volunteer to let go of her hand and she didn't make a move to pull it away, so we just walked hand in hand the rest of the way, talking about Jesus, God, her parents, and my experience in the sleep capsule. I told her about my upbringing, the good parts, the bad parts, the times I blamed Christians for doing the wrong things even when they had good intentions, and I told her about those people who claimed to be Christians, but did wrong with the worst of intentions.

"I hope you make a decision pretty soon," I said. "I think pretty soon most of the world will be lotus eaters, whether they want to be or not. Saul isn't going to tolerate people who don't join with him for very long. He wants the whole world on his side."

"I've already decided," she said quietly. "I want to know Jesus the way you do. With all that's happened to you, you are still calm and assured, like you know something the rest of us don't. I want that and I want to know I'm going to see my parents again."

So we sat there in the grass and both of us prayed. She prayed first, asking God to forgive her for not believing earlier and for everything she had done wrong. She asked him to give her the peace about the world that I had and she prayed for her Uncle Joseph, who wasn't likely to give up being a good Jew, as he called himself.

I prayed for both of them, along with everyone else I had met in the last couple of weeks. Had it really been a couple of weeks since I had woken out of my deep sleep? It was really kind of hard to tell because someone had messed with my mind at one point enough to make me think that a year and a half had passed and that I was going to be a father within a matter of months. That kind of mind game doesn't fade quickly and there were still times that I wondered which reality was really real. Wow, that was a mind blower. I still wondered even now if I might still be asleep in the capsule and all of this was a dream. It was possible, I suppose. But I had been able to control my dreams in the capsule, manipulate them, control them, and create entire worlds at a whim if I chose to. I couldn't control any of this and I felt like I was the one being manipulated by forces out of my control.

Still, Tye was here. Her hand was in my hand. We had both just prayed and I now knew that my future wife would be with me in Heaven someday. When that someday was and what kind of Hell on earth we would have to go through before then I didn't know, and further, I didn't care. As far as I was concerned, all was right with the world for the moment, even if the moment didn't last very long. And, naturally, it didn't.

CHAPTER NINE

We've all had those moments. I think everyone over the age of twelve has had at least one of those moments in their lifetime. Some of those under the age of twelve had them as well, but they were probably too young to really remember them and just let them pass away like so many other bad childhood memories. Tye and I had one of those moments as well.

We had just finished praying and were lying in the grass, just basking in the sunshine and enjoying each other's company. It was a wonderful Kodak moment and I told her so. She, of course, had absolutely no idea what I was talking about. Instead, she wanted to take a selfie. Which might have been fine, if it weren't for the sad fact that I was kind of a wanted man, a fugitive from the law. I almost felt like breaking out with a rendition of "Renegade" by Styx, but I was pretty sure that Tye was starting to fall for me and could just as easily fall away from me if she heard me sing. It's not that I'm a bad singer, but I've heard bats complain that it throws off their radar.

After a bit more basking, we headed back to the warehouse that had become my home. She couldn't wait to tell Joseph and hopefully convince him to believe as well. She was excited and filled with anticipation. I was excited just being around her. That kind of enthusiasm is totally contagious, so we both burst into the warehouse like a couple of schoolchildren with straight "A" report cards.

"Is that what you wear around men now?" Joseph asked before we had a chance to open our mouths. Most people, I've observed, will come automatically to their own defense, even when they know they are absolutely guilt of whatever crime they are accused of. It starts out as children, with their faces full of chocolate, their laps filled with crumbs, and a big smile on their little cherub faces, lying like a politician to their parents.

"No, of course I didn't eat the cookie. Why do I always get blamed?"

Tye was human. She had just experienced one of the most euphoric moments in her whole, short life, and Uncle Joseph was ready with a pea shooter to burst her bubble the minute he saw her. She slipped immediately into defensive mode.

"What's wrong with what I'm wearing?" she demanded. Actually, now that Uncle Joseph drew my attention to what she was wearing, I could see several things wrong with what she was wearing, starting with the fact that she wasn't really wearing much of anything at all. I grew up in the seventies with a couple of brothers who drove an orange Dodge Charger. They had a sister who was hotter than their car who wore a pair of cut off jean shorts. They looked like bell bottoms compared to the shorts Tye had on. They weren't so much shorts as much as they were a denim bikini bottom. Her top was some kind of hybrid between a halter and a tube top.

I should have seen it sooner. I really should have, but I had just left a society where nudity was more common than the cold. I had become desensitized to the human anatomy and it began to really bother me. It may seem like it would be great for a twenty year old man with raging hormones to be dropped into a society where anything goes and so everything was on display, but after just a short while, it all wears kind of thin. The problem was that I enjoyed the anticipation of Christmas more than I enjoyed Christmas itself.

Here's the thing that everyone needs to understand, a gift under the tree with just a bow covering it loses its appeal in just a short amount of time. Honestly, if you go by the tree on, let's say, the day after Thanksgiving and your gift is there with your name on it, but you know what it is, does it really have any appeal come Christmas morning?

I remember one Christmas where I actually had a family who cared for me and wanted me to have the best Christmas ever. Looking back, I realize that the best Christmas ever would have included adoption papers, but I'll let that slide for the time being. The point is, they wanted me to have a great Christmas. But they were also afraid that I'd be gone by Christmas. It had something to do with government paperwork, getting proper approval by the proper people, with, of course, everything signed and sealed in triplicate. I was just a kid enjoying a family for once, what did I know? It wasn't my job to keep up with that kind of stuff. It was my job to be a kid and at the time I was sorta good at it. Anyway, they gave me a bike. But because of their fear, I got the bike at the beginning of December.

For awhile I thought I had died and gone to Heaven, I was actually having my cake and eating it too. But by Christmas I was sick to death of cake. I could care less about cake, Cake made me vomit. I went into a diabetic coma because of cake.

Naturally, I got to stay with them through January before the government caught up with its own mistake and ruined the happiness of another child. So on Christmas morning, I got to open packages of underwear and socks with a reminder that my big Christmas present was sitting outside, rusting in the snow. It was a bummer, and it still is. If you know

what you're gonna get cause its walking around
unwrapped, or with just a bow and a streamer on it, do
you really want it when its offered to you? Probably
not as much as most people think. Trust me, I was
living the dream and it was quickly becoming a
nightmare.

"Nothing," said Joseph, "if you're working your
way through college." Ouch, that was a low blow.
Then, for some reason, I wondered if that vocation
even existed anymore. Would there be a need for
streetwalkers when everyone was giving it away? It
would be like owning a candy store when Willy
Wonka had just opened his factory for public
consumption.

"Blue likes what I'm wearing. Don't you Blue?"
Well, now that you mention it.

"Of course he likes it. You are walking around
like a dog in heat. What boy wouldn't like it?" Now
wait a minute. I may just be your average; run of the
mill twenty year old, but I could control my natural
urges. I had already proven as much with Jackee. She
wore a whole lot less than Tye did on a good day, and
she didn't have very many good days.

"I dress better than the kids I go to school with,"
she said defensively. If that was true, then I don't
know how any learning was accomplished. Then
again, the class she told me about focused on nineteen
eighties pop culture, so it wasn't exactly what I would
call a higher education. It was something like People

magazine, the National Enquirer, and Modern American History rolled into one package. Oh, and toss in a little of America's Top Forty for good measure.

"Naturally," he agreed, "since most of them don't wear anything at all."

"I'm just trying to fit in."

"Enough!" I shouted over their arguing. "Joseph, I know you love Tye as your own daughter. And Tye, I know you love your Uncle like a second dad. So why are you biting at each other like a couple of junkyard dogs?" That got their attention and quieted the arguing, which had gone from a normal tone of voice to the sonic boom of a jet airplane in less than five seconds. It was all I could do to be heard over them.

"Tye, don't you have something to tell your Uncle Joseph?" I switched from my commanding, demanding voice to one of gently prompting. It was something I learned from a drill sergeant in basic. Other drill sergeants all just one tone of voice, which happened to be very loud, but this gut accomplished more with a gently whisper than the rest of them yelling combined.

"I'm sorry, Uncle." That wasn't the thing I had in mind, but it definitely worked. For one thing, it set Joseph back on his heels. I had the feeling that they had this particular discussion on more than one occasion. I also surmised that all previous discussions ended with stomped feet, slammed doors, and days or weeks of either of them talking to one another. Tye had just signed the armistice while Uncle Joseph had his finger on the nuclear trigger. He didn't know what to do.

"I am sorry as well," he finally managed to say. "Please forgive an old man set in his ways. I wasn't raised in this kind of world and I don't want you to be either, but we have little choice."

They hugged, and hugged. And when they were through with that, they hugged some more. I guess they had some catching up to do. Or maybe they just liked hugging. I didn't have a whole lot of experience with good, decent families who actually cared for one another, so this was kind of new territory for me. Finally, they broke apart, well almost; they still held each other's hands.

"Uncle, I have news. I just accepted Yeshua. He has forgiven me and I will be with mom and dad in Heaven someday." She let it all rush out in one long sentence. I think she was eager to get it over for two reasons. First, she just had to tell someone, and there weren't many safe people to tell. Christians had all been rounded up and then disappeared. Shortly after that, Christianity was totally outlawed and anyone who even mentioned Jesus would be jailed, given a day in court, and then beheaded, not always in that order. I still didn't know why I was spared since I made no secret about what I believed. I could only assume that somebody somewhere had a reason for keeping me alive.

"No, this is impossible," Joseph cried. "I cannot lose you too." Then he turned on me and I thought for a minute he was going to try to hit me. "You did this. I brought you into our home and you corrupt this child." Okay, first of all, I'm pretty sure being twenty and in college means you are no longer a child. And second, I introduced her to Jesus. I didn't bring her home pregnant, drunk, and strung out on cocaine or heroin. And, thirdly, just for good measure, no one lost her. In fact, no one could lose her now. Joseph was the one who was lost, but just too blind to know it. That had to change and soon.

"Joseph," I began, "have you had a chance to look through the scriptures? Have you honestly read Daniel and not seen prophecy fulfilled in Yeshua? Have you read the story of Joseph and not seen the suffering servant who saves all of Israel? Not to mention Ruth and Boaz, the kinsman redeemer."

"Yes, yes, I have seen all of these things you talk of, and many more. I know, and I see, but I don't know how to believe. These are dangerous times."

"There have always been dangerous times," I countered. "The early church was full of Sons of Abraham who lived in dangerous times, but they didn't let the danger override their faith in the creator of Heaven and earth. They knew in whom they believed and were convinced he could keep them." I don't know if my words were having any affect on him. I really hope not. I know that sounds strange, but I didn't want to convince him or anyone else of anything because I didn't want their faith to be in me or any answers I could provide. I was just another idiot who figured out the truth one day too late. If they had faith, it needed to be in God, not in me.

"I want to believe," he finally stated. "If Yeshua can cause this stubborn child to apologize, then He is indeed a worker of miracles." And so, for the second time that day, we prayed, this time with Joseph.

"What now?" Tye asked. "I can't go back to class." I had already thought of that, but I didn't have enough information. I was, or had been, an intelligence analyst. But now I was completely out of my league. I didn't have any intelligence to analyze.

"Fill me in on the world," I stated. "Give me the Reader's Digest version of who, what, and where." They both looked at me with blank expressions, so I elaborated a little. "Tell me who all the players are. Are there others like you, or like you were before. You know, people who aren't Christian, but who also don't have the perfect bodies."

"Isn't my body perfect enough for you?" Tye teased. Joseph shot her a look and she quickly stopped. I continued with my questions.

"If there are other people like you, where are

they? Do some livde close to the others like y'all do, or do they live separate lives, away from these types of societies? And, finally, at least for now, what are our assets and liabilities if we have to go on the run? Can we even hope to escape if they have eyes and ears everywhere?"

So they began to fill in the bits and pieces that had been left out of my information gathering so far. Alright, so it was more like chunks and boulders that had been left out, but it wasn't like I had a library available to me. I had the internet, which was about as reliable as Old Aunt Harriet gossiping over the fence, and just about as informative. If I needed to know about cat videos or fashion or the latest buzz about who was who in Hollywood, then the computer and the internet were my best friend, but if I wanted reliable information about the world around me like who my friends might be and who my enemies were, well that was a different story.

And it was no wonder. One of the first things Joseph told me was that the media was controlled by the government, which was global, with Saul in charge. The United States still had a President, just as England still had a Queen and Parliament and just as every other country had its own version of a puppet ruler, but Saul was the great puppet master of them all.

As far as anyone could tell, Europe had wholeheartedly signed on with Saul from the beginning. They welcomed his rule as benign and beneficial. And it was no wonder, since he was offering them a sort of eternal life, with only one string attached, and it was a nearly invisible nylon thread that no one paid much attention to in the beginning. By the time anyone caught on, it was too late. They were totally under the control of their new puppet master, only now instead of a couple of hundred puppets in government, the entire population was in his control. Again, no one cared because for the most part, he let them do what they wanted because it fit into his plan for them to do so. People were free to express themselves in any way they wanted, in any form or fashion they chose. They were free from the so called sexual repression that came with societal conventions. They were free to give themselves to drugs, alcohol or any other mind altering chemical. They were free to do as they please because their bodies were almost eternal because of the nanobots placed inside of them. Never mind that those same nanobots connected themselves to their brain stems and used their minds as supplemental computers for his mainframe supercomputer, and never mind that he altered their perceptions of space, reality, and even time. It was all good as long as they had their self-healing bodies and could lose themselves in their lust.

And, of course, the Unites States quickly followed suit in almost every fashion, except there were a few holdouts. For one, there were survivalist groups who considered Saul and his promises of a new Utopia part of an alien conspiracy. Some of them blamed the Christians, although Saul was the first one to suggest, and then later command, that the world round up and arrest Christians. It was plain to anyone listening that he only did that because he was really in league with them and somehow he had managed to help them escape, probably on rockets to the moon.

Other survivalists though, simply wanted to be left alone. They didn't see everything as a vast right, left, or right down the middle conspiracy, but they didn't want to join the rest of society in debauchery. They weren't Christians, but they still had a common decency and some common sense. They recognized that nothing in this life is free and that although you might not get a bill today, it is definitely coming with interest compounded on a daily basis.

And then there were the Jews and the Moslems, both groups exempted from the need to have the new bodies in order to join with Saul's society. The Jews were exceptional, according to what passed for historians, because they were the original people of the Book and as such were the first covenantal people of God. Saul argued that although all gods were equally valid, since God himself was eternal and could display himself any way he chose, that the God of Israel was the original, so to speak. That meant the Jews were off limits to the persecution that others in the world might face if they didn't conform to the new society.

Moslems were basically in the same category as the Jews. Although their religion didn't come along until thousands of years after the Jews first appeared in covenant with God, they were the wild olive branch grafted in, and as such also enjoyed special privileges and exemptions from rules and taxes.

There were Christians, or at least it was rumored there was. I thought there might be for a couple of reasons. First, many of those conspiracy groups and survivalists had their roots in Christianity. Christians hadn't trusted any form of government for decade. Some of those, most in fact, had disappeared in the rapture with others who had been jailed. Those left behind quickly converted to true faith in Jesus Christ and were consequently hunted down like animals.

The rest of the groups, although technically outlawed, were still allowed to trade with those in Saul's society. Although, according to Joseph, that was soon to stop. It was rumored that only those who belonged to the one world form of government would be allowed to buy, sell, and trade. Commerce was to go through governmental channels, and those channels alone. Of course there would be black market trading. There always was, but it would be getting harder to do once the new regulations were in place. Those regulations exempted, for a time anyway, both Jew and Moslems.

This meant that we had to move quickly. For one thing, Saul had eyes and ears almost everywhere.

Every one of those with the new bodies, his new society, served as unwitting intelligence gatherers when they downloaded information every night. But on top of that, there were cameras almost everywhere, and where there weren't camera, there was satellites. Every intelligence gathering entity, from the CIA to MI-6 now served Saul. I guess technically I should say they served the new world order and its government, but since Saul was the benevolent dictator over all of it, it was just easier and more truthful to say Saul.

So we had two basic choices, neither of them really good. Of course the first thing we had to do was to get on the move. The question was which direction to travel. The survivalist groups welcomed almost everyone into their cliques, as long as they were willing to work and serve their leaders, but many of them had their own dictators who weren't necessarily so benevolent. And many of them also traded information for favors with Saul and his society. It would be tricky, but Joseph thought he knew which groups might be trusted, at least for a time. That would grant them breathing room to regroup, rethink and replenish supplies.

The other alternative was much trickier. There were underground Christian groups. They didn't necessarily welcome visitors and guests because no one could be trusted. For them it was a matter of survival for them to stay underground and to stay secret. No one knew, except maybe for Saul, where any of these groups were, or if they really existed. Their lives would be that of hunted animals. Finally, after hearing everything, then working and reworking everything in my mind, chewing it over mentally like a cow with its cud, I came to a decision and hoped beyond hope that Tye and Joseph would listen to reason.. Then again, my plan wasn't all that reasonable and was based more on guilt, emotion, and downright shame more than on logic and reason. But I felt led to follow through with it.

"I think we need to seek out the Christians," I said. "They are the only ones we can really trust at this point to not turn us in." Joseph and Tye agreed, which meant so far so good. It was the next point that would be a point of contention, probably with both of them, but especially with Tye. It's funny, we had only known each other for a little while, but in that time we had fallen deeply in love. It began with holding hands on our walk, or maybe that was just the physical seal of what had already taken place in our hearts. Now there you go, here I was in love and I was getting all poetic and emotional. Maybe it was because we realized there was little time. Even if we managed to get to a place of safety, it was only a matter of time before the tribulation began in earnest, and then our time was really short. More than likely we all faced beheading.

The funny thing was, it didn't seem to bother any of us. We knew that by placing our faith in Jesus, we were putting our necks on the chopping block, but it didn't matter. For us it was better to die quickly physically than to live and die eternally without Jesus. It was really a no brainer. I just couldn't figure out why everyone else didn't see it so plainly. I mean, I could kind of understand why those with the new bodies didn't jump at the chance. After all, in their way of thinking, they were already living eternally in a self made paradise. Why would they trade that for several years of persecution and the hope of an eternal resurrection? They would have to trade something they held in their hand for the hope of something that couldn't even be seen. Of course, that kind of thinking wasn't helping me when it came to what I needed to do.

On the other hand, why didn't people who rejected Saul then accept Jesus? Again, I could kind of excuse some of them. There were still Moslems, Buddhists, Hindus, and others that held on to their own beliefs. Saul made it easy for them to do since he announced that God could be reached by any means. As long as you were sincere in your belief, all roads led to Heaven. So what if you worshipped a head of lettuce and it rotted? Could you then swap out heads and still be sincere in your beliefs and would that get you to Nirvana, Paradise, Valhalla, or whatever you call eternal bliss? It didn't make a lot of sense to me.

Okay, so that basically leaves those with no beliefs. If they had any inkling of what the rapture was about, and there had been a ton of books, videos, movies and other media undertakings to show the rapture, then why didn't you recognize it when it happened right in front of your face? And if you recognized it, then why didn't you recognize the God who prophesied that the rapture would take place? How could you be so blind? And that was it, wasn't it? They were blind. The Bible said so. It said that the god of this world, who at this moment was in essence Saul, blinded the eyes of people so they couldn't see the truth when it smacked them right between their eyes. Besides, I remembered something else about the end times. I remembered that at some point God gets so fed up with folks that he sends out a strong delusion that they might believe a lie. And I'll be a monkey's uncle if He didn't do just that. The whole thing with Jesus being an alien and all of his followers being aliens set to take over the world was one big lie sold by Saul, but in essence its origin was in Heaven. God allowed it because people had chosen to listen to lies for a long time and God finally just let them have what they wanted any way. It's like the kid who whines and whines for a cookie or candy or some other kind of treat, and the parent gets sick of it enough to let them eat sweets till they puke. Never happened to me, but I've had friends who say they've gone through it and I believe them because they wouldn't even eat Halloween candy.

"How will we find them?" Joseph wondered. That was a doggone good question, but one I think I had the answer to. It was times like these that I really appreciated being drug, sometimes kicking and screaming, to Sunday school and Vacation Bible

School. It was at one VBS that we learned about early Christian symbols and how the early church used them to guide other Christians. It was kind of like an early version of the Underground Railroad that led slaves to freedom.

"Look for symbols that the early church used. I bet they're still using them." I took a stick and drew on the ground a few of the symbols I remembered from that program, including a fish, an anchor, the Greek alpha and omega, and some others. I had them each study them and commit them to memory. Now came the part I had dreaded.

"I need y'all to trust me, and to trust God." I added that last part because I thought that maybe it lent a bit of authority to what I was about to suggest, but I really meant it. I was sure God was leading me to do what I was about to do or I wouldn't have considered it. Well, I might have considered it, but I would have dismissed it because of my new love for Tye.

"What is it?" Tye asked with apprehension.

"I need you to go on ahead. Leave me clues about which way you are going and I'll track you and catch up to you later."

"Later?" she asked. "How much later?"

"Just as soon as I've done what I need to do," I replied cryptically. I knew I had to tell them what I was about to do and I also knew they would try to argue me out of it, but I really had no choice. Love, honor and my commitment to God all told me what I had to do.

"Spit it out, boy," Joseph demanded. "I think I know what you are wanting, and although I see the danger of it, I agree with you." Whoa! I didn't see that coming, but I was glad that at least Tye would be outvoted. Of course that wouldn't matter much because it was two men versus one woman and men were pig-headed fools who wouldn't know how to wipe their noses or their behinds without women teaching them. She probably was right.

"I have to go back and witness to Jackee," I finally said. "I know it's dangerous and I know she'll probably betray me, but I can't leave without trying to reach her with the gospel. If I had been a stronger Christian when I was with her, I would have already done it, but I was caught up in all the lies and didn't tell her the truth."

"No," Tye said. "You don't owe that woman anything. She tried to seduce you and she'll do it again. And this time she might succeed. I won't have my husband in the bed of another woman, especially a..." I stopped her before she could finish her thought. But I knew what she was going to say and it wasn't pretty. It was the truth, to be sure, but it wasn't pretty.

"Tye, I love you. I have from the moment I saw you. And I will for all of eternity. That's a promise.

But I have to go. I have no choice. This is as much the hand of God as my own heart. I don't ask you to like it or even really accept it. I just ask that you trust me. And I'll say it again, trust God." She turned to her uncle for support, but he was on my side. He understood the pain I was in. I had missed the opportunity to witness to someone who had saved my life, who, although falsely, carried my baby. I knew that was false, a lie concocted by Saul for some mysterious reason, but it still felt real in my heart. False memories, even when you know they are false, are still memories.

"Go," she finally relented. "And I will forgive you if you end up in her bed. I know how deceitful those people can be. But I won't forgive you if you end up dying before you've had the chance to become my husband and provide us with a strong daughter."

"Don't you mean son?" I asked.

"You can have a dozen of each," she said. "But the daughter comes first."

We talked awhile longer, finalizing plans, agreeing on symbols to look for and symbols for them to leave so I could find them. We gathered supplies and gathered what little wits we had about us. Finally Joseph wrote out directions for me to follow through the tunnel system so that I'd be able to locate the apartment Jackee had shared with me. Knowing my sense of direction, I'd probably come out ahead of them in the woods someplace.

I kissed Tye long and hard. She returned my kiss eagerly and hungrily. I wanted that one kiss to last forever, but nothing on this earth does, so I just had to look forward to a new Heaven and new earth. Until then I looked forward to a restless night's sleep, another morning, and a mission that would more than likely lead to my death, which meant no forgiveness from Tye.

CHAPTER TEN

Before leaving, I had another talk with Joseph. He was well versed in the Old Testament and because he was Jewish, he was allowed to keep a copy for study. No one had any of the New Testament scriptures and while I had listened to them for years, I didn't have them memorized, so most of our knowledge of end time prophecy came from Joseph's understand of books like Daniel and Ezekiel.

"I still don't get why the tribulation didn't begin with the rapture," I said. "I thought that was the trigger that would set off the countdown for the end of the world."

"I'm sure most people thought so. But our ways are not God's ways and His thoughts are not our thoughts. God often does things in unexpected ways, many of them we don't recognize until after they are done."

"Like sending a Messiah through a young virgin engaged to a carpenter?" I asked.

"Yes, exactly like that," he said with a broad smile. Then his expression turned melancholic. "I only wish I had listened to my sister when she told me of Yeshua. I refused to listen after she married that goyim." I knew the term could be used pretty much as a curse word, and I just bet that when Joseph used it to talk about his brother-in-law earlier, it was just that. But now he had accepted Jesus as his savior and the word was just another used to describe all of us who weren't fortunate enough to be born Jewish so I wasn't the least bit offended.

"It wasn't your time," I answered. "You were needed here. I needed you here, so blame me instead of blaming yourself."

"Then I will," he said, laughing and slapping his big hand across my back. "And I will most certainly blame you if you do not return to marry my niece. She has been the only sunshine in my dark world, but do not tell her I said so."

"You ought to tell her yourself," I told him.

"Yes," Tye agreed, "you should tell me yourself. Joseph stood up awkwardly, his face red flushed with embarrassment. They hugged again, still making up for years of distant love and a chilled relationship.

"We should all be going," I said. I wasn't eager to be separated from Tye or Joseph, for that matter, but I wanted them to be far away from here, and I had things to do that really didn't need to wait either. Tye came over to me and through her arms around me in a tight embrace.

"You better come back to me," she sobbed. "I've never been in love before and I'm not going to lose my first one." What could I say? I didn't want to lose her either. Had I been in love before? No, I really don't think so. There were other women in my life in the past, but I didn't have much of a past to fill up with men, women or anything else. There might have been a case or two of puppy love sometime or another, but if there was, I couldn't think of their names. Shoot, at the moment, with Tye's arms around me, her body pressed hard against mine, her sweet body odor filling my nostrils, and her hair tickling my nose, I had a hard time thinking of my own name. We finally pulled away from each other. They grabbed their backpacks of provisions and I turned to walk the other way. Then I turned back, grabbed and kissed her one more time before going on my way.

The directions Joseph gave me were thorough, well thought out and detailed. I got lost twice before finding my through the tunnels and back on the city streets. The closest he could get me was about ten blocks from Jackee's apartment. I could have taken a cab the rest of the way, but I decided to let the walk there clear my head and prepare me for what I hoped would be the sales pitch of a lifetime.

I noticed several people watching me as I walked along the street. I tried to be inconspicuous, but when you're the only fully clothed person walking on a street full of nude and mostly nude people, you have a tendency to stick out just a little. I don't think I was being paranoid. Besides, even paranoid people have some real enemies, and I already knew that I had some real enemies out there. I also knew that same enemy could use the eyes and ears of every person here as his personal spies. I wondered how that worked. Did they have someone monitoring different people at different times, the way you might look over a bank of monitors at a department store or museum? Or did they just see what they wanted after the nightly download. Somehow that didn't seem practical. Maybe when they saw something out of place, an alarm went off and they began a download then.

In just a short amount of time, I noticed that it seemed like more than eyes were following me. Some of the pedestrians were beginning to fall in behind me. But when I turned back to look, they were all busy acting casual. I began to feel like a spy or a wanted criminal in one of those old, film noir, black and white movies. I was Peter Lorre on the run from Orson Welles, on my way to see Rita Hayworth. It was funny that all those old actors and actresses should pop into my mind just now, but I had watched a slew of those old films. One of my fosters was a movie buff who had a keen interest in that genre.

Just before I got to the street where Jackee's apartment was, I took a right away from her place. Then I circled the block just to see if I spotted anyone taking the lap with me, but it seemed by tail had gotten bobbed somewhere along the way, so maybe I was just being paranoid, or maybe that was a conspiracy rumor spread about me by my enemies. Either way, I made my way up to her apartment. If they followed, so be it. I wasn't going to let a bunch of nudist keep me from my mission.

She answered the door on the first knock. The sight of her nearly took my breath away. She was stunning, with all the right curves in all the right places and absolutely nothing between my eyes and her skin to interfere with my vision. Before I could speak, she ran at me, through her arms around my neck and jumped up. I was forced to either take her in my arms or fall backwards with her. I chose to wrap my arms around her and walk myself and her back into the apartment.

"Blue," she cried, "I've missed you so terribly. I was worried absolutely sick with grief at the thought of losing you." Then she buried her face in my shoulder for just a moment before turning her luscious lips into my ear. "You shouldn't have come back. They're looking for you." I turned into her ears. I never realized how perfect they were. But then why shouldn't they be, since everything else on her curvaceous body was.

"They know I'm here. It's too late to turn back now. Can you get dressed real quick? I hate to impose, but I need to talk to you about something real important and you're just a bit of a distraction."

"Blue, you say the nicest things to a girl. I'll throw on a t-shirt and maybe even some shorts since you asked so nice." She came out a few minutes later in a teddy with matching lacy shorts. It wasn't much of an improvement. In fact it may have been even more attractive and more distractive than the total nudity, but I had to hurry and there was no telling what else she had in her closet if I asked her to change.

"Jackee," I started, "you know I never tried to hide that I was a Christian. I understand that's against the law, but if it is, so be it. I would rather stand with God against the world rather than with God against the world."

"Blue, I wish you wouldn't talk about such things. I'm supposed to turn you in. And even if I don't, they're probably already listening." I had thought about that. I wondered if she knew that they might be listening through her ears and watching him at this moment through her eyes. It was a disturbing thought, but one that I'd already dealt with in my head. I had things to say and I needed to say them before the Gestapo or the Secret Police or whatever they called their good squad here.

"I don't care," I said with absolute assurance in my heart. I was confident that what I needed to do, I could."Jackee, I want you to accept Jesus as your savior. I want you to ask him to forgive you of your sins. Jackee, I want you to be in Heaven with me."

She was crying. No she was more than crying. She was absolutely sobbing, with deep, heavy sobs. Her chest heaved up and down with each cry.

"Oh, Blue. I wish I could. I really wish I could. I want to be with you, too. I think I love you, Blue." That was a bit awkward. I had no idea how to respond to that. In my mind, we had been together less than a month. It was really hard to say for sure, because they had messed with my mind and perceptions of time and space so much that I had a hard time distinguishing reality from their version of fantasy at times. In her mind, though, we had been together for over a year. It was hard to say what kind of experiences they had placed in her psyche. She had memories of the two of us doing things that we hadn't done, of me saying things that I hadn't said. It was unnerving, and even more so because in some ways I loved her too. But I also loved Tye deeper in the few hours we had together than I could love Jackee in a lifetime.

"Why can't you?" I finally asked. "Ask Jesus to forgive you and he will. I know it sounds too simple to be true, but it is. He forgave me while I was between worlds in sleep. Surely he would save you if you ask." The tears flowed again. Not big heavy sobs, but small, sweet, quiet whimpers.

"I can't, Blue, because I belong to Saul. I'm his creation and he won't let me go. Besides, I chose my destiny when I chose this body. I knew the truth before I became what I am, but I didn't care. I chose the world and temporary pleasures over eternity. I still have those memories in there, buried somewhere under everything else." She laid her head over on my shoulders and quietly cried and cried. It was the most real emotion I had ever seen from her and she was the most beautiful I had ever seen her, It was her openness and vulnerability that brought out her true beauty instead of the artificial saccharin sweetness that she had been displaying. After a few minutes, she recovered enough to speak.

"Blue, you have to leave and leave now. If you don't, I literally won't be responsible for what I might do. They'll control me and I won't be able to stop them." Well, that answered that question for me. I had wondered if she knew she was being controlled and manipulated. I guess she at least had some sense of it, enough to warn me that I was in danger. But I couldn't leave, not yet. I needed to be sure that I had done everything I could to tell her about Jesus.

"Please, Jackee, won't you please try? I don't want to lose you. You saved my life and I owe you more than I can say."

"I want to Blue, I honestly do, but I told you, I decided my destiny years ago. Now, please, if you care for me at all, please leave before something terrible happens."

I was getting up to leave when the front door

burst open and three large men came busting through. The first one rushed right at me and I stood there, letting him come. At the last second, I cut right and gave him a good shove over the couch as he passed by me. The second guy was a little more cautious. He through a hard right at me from just above his shoulder. I ducked underneath it, and slammed my shoulder into his chest, knocking the wind out of him. Between his forward momentum and my shoulder, I think he busted a couple of ribs. While I was under him, I came up hard and landed a fist against his jaw, knocking at least a couple of teeth out.

The third guy hung way back, reappraising the situation. No doubt he had been told that they had not only superior numbers, but superior bodies and training, but the way I had them figured is that they probably never fought much. What would be there to fight over? Women gave their bodies away, and if they chose to swim upstream against the tide of nature, well the guys gave it away too. There was booze, drugs, and other forms of intoxication for the taking. So, other than fighting for the sake of fighting, they only had training. That was kind of like reading a drivers manual and then thinking you could get behind the wheel of a car and take off.

I lunged forward, hoping to call his bluff. Then I suddenly fell back, hoping to pull him in to the confrontation, and that's when the lights went out. But how was that possible? He was still in front of me; the other two were still on the floor recovering from their wounds. Why was I suddenly falling to the floor and seeing stars? Just before my eyes closed for good, they saw what had closed them. It was Jackee, holding a statue of a naked Venus de Milo. And then there was darkness.

When my eyes opened again, I knew exactly where I was. Well, not exactly maybe, but I had a good idea. When you are raised as a foster kid and bounced from home to home, especially when you bounce pretty hard in some of them, you learn to recognize what police stations look like. I had that going for me, along with the handcuffs and shackles to use as clues. I may not be Columbo, but I can figure out a few things on my own. Oh, and one more thing, the dumb brute in front of me was a hard-nosed, hard headed cop looking to make good by breaking me. Even with the nearly perfect body that everyone had here, this guy simply screamed donuts and bacon. Yeah, I know that's a stereotype, but all of those stereotypes start somewhere. It's like they say, in all myths and legends there is a kernel of truth somewhere. I still ain't figured how a guy can have a set of six pack abs and a pot belly from too many six packs, but this bozo managed it somehow.

"So sleeping beauty decided to wake up," he snarled.

"Shoot," I said, "I thought I was still sleeping and you were the troll in my nightmare. No, wait, never mind, the troll wasn't as ugly as you."

"Wiseguy, huh?" Okay, was that taught in the police academy? Some punk smarts off and the first thing out of your detective mouth is, "Wiseguy, huh?" I was flashing back to the film noir thing from earlier. This guy was no Bogie. He was more that character actor who nobody can ever remember the name of. Then when he dies, they play a marathon of all three of his movies.

"Yeah, see, I'm a wiseguy, see." It wasn't the best Cagney anyone had ever done, but maybe it wasn't the worst either. Maybe, and then again, maybe it was. I'm thinking it was cause the Bogie man came flying across the table to get in my face. Whew, call the Geneva Convention, cause I'm pretty doggone sure that his breath qualified for biological or chemical weapons, or more likely both. Did he have garlic and onions with every meal? At least I knew I wasn't being interrogated by a vampire.

"We know someone helped you escape." Duh, really? Some guy wakes up from forty years in the past, has brains scrambled like breakfast eggs, eludes the authorities for days and is only caught cause he wants to see a friend get saved, and he figures out I had help. No wonder they made him detective. I'm thinking Barney Fife wasn't available. I knew the next thing out of his mouth was gonna be the whole tell us who it was thing. "Who helped you? Tell us who and we'll take it easy on you." Wow, did I call that one or what? I didn't know how much chain this guy was gonna give me, and to be honest, I didn't really care.

As long as they were focusing on me, they weren't focusing on Tye and Joseph. So if this guy was gonna give me some chain, then I was going to yank his.

"Fine," I said with a sigh. "Fine, have it your way." I hung my head as in shame. I wanted to play this right. If I gave in too quickly, he'd smell a rat. After all, I had already established his formidable skills as a detective. I wanted to give him some names, but not yet. "How about something to drink first? That blow to my head is killing me. And how about some aspirin or something?"

"Aww," he mocked, "do you need a pillow, too? And maybe a blanket or a teddy bear."

"Hey," I shouted, "how would you feel if the woman you loved betrayed you and knocked you in the head with the statue of a naked woman? Maybe you'd want something for the pain too."

"That's why I don't tie myself down," he grinned a big wolfish grin. "I sleep with all the ladies so none of them can let me down." It was a good thing that nobody held themselves back from anyone; otherwise this guy would probably tie himself a good knot and hang himself with it.

"Yeah, well, what can I say? I fooled around and fell in love." My apologies to Elvin Bishop, wherever he is.

"What you can say it who helped you to escape. I

need names or things are gonna get rough around here." Wow! Another line from the bad policeman's manual on how to interrogate prisoners and make friends.

"There were two of them," I said. So far, I wasn't lying, but the real fun was about to begin. I just hoped six pack here didn't catch on to things very quickly. He didn't seem the type to catch anything, really, whether it was quickly or not.

"Names," he repeated. "I need names."

"The first guys name was Rotch. Funny name, huh?"

"Rotch?" he said, "Is that Jewish?"

"How should I know? He grabbed me out of the club on Creator's day and led me out front. Said his name was Mike. He introduced me to a guy driving a big white van, the kind that makes deliveries."

"All right," he said. "Now we're getting someplace. One guy was named Rotch, Micheal. Who was the other guy?"

"Not Micheal, just Mike," I corrected. "The other guys name was Nuss. I think his first name was Uri. I think he might be German. He might be Jewish too. Sounds like a Jewish name, doesn't it?"

Garlic breath got up, walked over to the door and pressed an intercom button. The voice on the other end squawed something at him and he responded by giving them the names I had given him. He also told them to be looking for a large, white delivery van.

"We have two fugitives we're looking for. One is named Nuss, Uri. That's Uri Nuss. If you find Uri Nuss, please call the authorities immediately."

I was dangling a carrot in front of him. That carrot was nothing more than some dog poop painted orange, but he hadn't figured that out yet.

"The other man we are looking for is Mike Rotch. I repeat, Mike Rotch. Check all the data bases for Mike Rotch and Uri Nuss, last seen in a big white van. I repeat, we are looking for Mike Rotch and Uri Nuss, last seen together in a big white van."

The laughter started slow, as if people couldn't believe what they were hearing, or maybe they just didn't get it. Who knows if people in this decade have any kind of sense of humor or not? But I guess they did, because the laughter that started out as a gentle wave soon swelled into a massive force of wind and water. It roared through the police station, and finally drifted into the interrogation room where I was going to get the tar beat out of in about five minutes when he figured out those names were false, but funny. Well, funny to me anyways. I don't think he was gonna find them too funny, but stupid detectives with garlic breath and six pack abs that come from real six packs aren't known for their great sense of humor. It took about five minute and several more calls over the intercom before he realized that I had played him.

Now, I've never really been afraid of dying. Zeke used to say that it wasn't the destination that bothered him, it was the journey. Even before I was saved, death didn't hold much of a sway over me. That's because I was young and stupid. It's not much of an excuse, but it's the best I got. And even if it's not the best excuse, it certainly is a common one because I've seen a lot of people use it, mostly under twenty punks like me. Now, however, I didn't fear death because I knew where I was going. The journey, however, still bothered me, mostly because I knew the taxi I was gonna take was the fists of an irate detective who couldn't find either Mike Rotch or Uri Nuss with both hands. But those hands balled into fists were about to do a number on my face and body.

The first punch landed squarely in the center of my face. I was handcuffed with my hands behind me and my feet were shackled to the floor, so the best I could hope for was that I might pummel his fists with my face and that at some point he might get a knick from one of my many broken ribs. I've felt pain before. I've been beat up before. You lose a lot of fights before you start winning any consistently. But I've never been so totally helpless to defend myself. I should have seen it coming. I know others had seen it. I had been warned over and over about the possibility of someone beating me senseless. I don't think they ever considered that it might be in a police station while I was strapped down and defenseless, but others had warned me. Mr. Jackson, my eighth grade guidance counselor told me once that I had a disease called, "aperi os suum". I thought that sounded terrible and wondered what it was, was there a cure for it, and was I gonna die from it. He told me that it was Latin for open mouth disease, that the only cure known was a good butt whooping from time to time and that I probably would die from it. Thanks a lot, Mr. Jackson, wherever you are. You were a prophet and didn't even know it.

I was hoping beyond hope that I would just pass out. I couldn't do anything else except hope, and pray. The prayers were silent, though, because I think my jaw was already broken. Either way, my mouth wasn't working anymore.

Just as I did pass out, the door flew open and in walked the best looking man I had ever seen. He didn't so much walk as float, like an angel. I'm not gay or anything like that. In fact, I could look at this guy and appreciate his good looks because I knew I wasn't gay. But I might have fallen in love with him anyway, because as soon as he walked in, the beating stopped. He had my vote as guardian angel.

"Detective, what part of I don't want him harmed didn't you understand?" the angel asked.

"Sir, I do understand. But he just kept pushing and pushing. I lost control sir. It will never happen again."

"I do understand. Mr. Blue can be very trying. He has tried my patience over and over again. It can be quite aggravating." Wow, I didn't know I was such a popular guy. Mr. Jackson would be proud of me. I had not only angered a detective past the point of losing control, but I had also tried the patience of the handsomest man I had ever seen. I'm really not gay, but this guy was extremely good looking and I didn't mind admitting that. "And you are right. This will never happen again." At that point, handsome guy pulled a gun from somewhere and shot the detective between his eyes. He hit the floor with a blank stare.

"We'll clean up," another voice said. I didn't see the source, but it must have been some more policemen. Or maybe it was part of the angelic entourage. I didn't know and I didn't care.

"He was a Christian," the angel announced, and everyone took it for granted that the abusive detective was indeed a Christian. As such, he would have his head cut off. I wondered if he could have recovered otherwise. Joseph said the nanobots allowed people to heal from most wounds. Would that include a gunshot wound between the eyes? I guess he was never gonna find out because part of the entourage came in and drug the body out, promising to be sure his head would be taken from his body.

"What about him?" someone asked.

"Have him taken to a healer and taken care of," the angel commanded. "I will see him again soon."

With that he walked out, handing his gun to one of his lackeys as he turned around. Then he was gone again, and I was being laid on a gurney to be taken to a "healer"

For the second time that day, I woke up to a whole new world. I was told by some of my teachers that I woke up in a new world every day. Today I was proving those people right.

I woke up with lips being pressed to mine. They were sweet, soft and luscious. I wanted to drink them in like a man drinks in water after weeks in the desert. They were tastier than anything that I had ever had in my mouth before and I wanted to taste more, so I pressed out my tongue into her mouth and she welcomed it while at the same time granting me hers.

"Tye," I sighed during a break. The lips stopped and the body sprang away from me. It wasn't Tye? Then who?

"The name's Jackee, in case you've forgotten," she said icily.

"I'm sorry," I answered lamely. "I guess I was dreaming."

"Well, from now on, dream about me when you are with me. She may be your wife, but I'm your concubine and it's my turn to have you this week. You're mine when you're with me. Understand? Now come on, sleepyhead, you've got a show to do."

"A show?" I asked.

"You really did have too much to drink last night. Don't tell me you can't remember performing your one man show based on growing up in the seventies."

I did remember, didn't I? How could anyone forget something like that? I was famous. People around the world loved me. I had several CD's out , most of them still on the best selling list. My podcast had millions of hits, with more coming everyday. I had everything a man could ask for. I was rich, I was famous. I had the love of the two most beautiful women on earth. It was almost too good to be true.

Whoa! Hold the horses. It wasn't almost too good to be true. It was totally too good to be true. I didn't have a podcast. I wasn't putting on a show in a little bit. There were no CD's. Tye wasn't my wife, and Jackee wasn't my concubine. Someone was playing with my head again and I was getting sick and tired of it. I stood up suddenly, which was a mistake, because my pants were nowhere to be seen. I snatched up some of the covers and headed for the door.

"Send them in," I demanded.

"What are you talking about?" she asked innocently. "There is no one to send in."

"Don't play with me!" I was getting angry. I was angry with whoever kept playing with my memories. I was angry with her for her part in it. And most of all I was angry with myself for falling for it, again. Most of all, I was doubly angry with myself for wanting to fall for it. Her kiss still lingered at the edge of my lips as much as her body lingered at the edge of my mind. I really wanted to hit someone. That thought triggered something in me. It was the truth. I had been beaten, almost to death. And then the angel saved me, had me healed, and then he did this to me. He was the one who was the great deceiver. Didn't the Bible warn that the devil looked like an angel of light?

I found my pants and made my way to the door, leaving Jackee behind with her mouth left agape. I was almost out the door when I heard her speak, but it wasn't her voice. Well, it wasn't exactly her voice. The tone was there, but it was flat, metallic.

"Stop," the voice commanded. "Wait here to be picked up."

"And if I choose to leave? Are you going to conk me in the head again?"

"No, I'll kill Jackee. Either stay here, or she dies."

"Do what you want. She means nothing to me," I lied.

"As you wish," the voice said. Jackee reached down, picked up a knife that was on the nightstand, and held it to her throat, right against her jugular. I grabbed the doorknob and turned slightly to see what might happen. She started to press the knife into her flesh deeper. I twisted the knob and the knife started scraping across the flesh. With only a little more pressure, there would be arterial spurting and Jackee would be dead within minutes. I saw fear in her eyes. She knew what was happening, but was powerless to stop it. I was the only one who could stop it, and only by allowing myself to be captured. I had come here to save Jackee, or more precise, to see Jesus save her. Now, though, I was leading her to her death and that without Jesus.

"Stop," I cried. The knife came away from the throat, but was still within an inch of pressing back into the skin. "I'll do whatever you want."

"Good, I knew you'd see things my way. Jackee will be fine now. You've saved her life. Maybe once you've done as I asked, I will allow the two of you your time together. I am not a monster, you know." But I didn't know. I didn't know anything of the sort. He held a knife to a womans throat just to get his way. He played with my mind like a chalkboard that could be erased and rewritten on at will. He was a total monster, but he was totally in control for the time being.

Men arrived shortly after that, two of them were the ones I had beaten earlier that day. I could tell they were itching to abuse me, but they held themselves back. I guess the story of the detective with his brain splattered the entire interrogation room wall. That kind of surprised me. I thought there would have been a brain wipe of the entire event. Then again, maybe I only assumed they knew. It might have been that the episode was wiped, but that the Saul allowed a fragment to remain as a warning. It was really hard to tell.

"No need for rough stuff, boys," I said, raising my hands in surrender, "I'm coming along peacefully."

"It's a good thing," one of them said. I think it was the one who went sailing over the couch. "Because you won't catch us off guard again."

I stepped forward hard, lunging in his direction with a punch to the gut, and then pulled back at the last minute and raised my hands again. He almost sprawled backwards over the coffee table. It was rude, I know. It was also uncalled for and totally annoying and irritating. In other words, it was textbook me just being me.

CHAPTER ELEVEN

I was led to spacious office. Or at least I think it was an office. It had all the trappings of being an office. There was a big oak desk, some file cabinets, a computer workstation and other assorted office furniture. But there was also a very comfortable and very large couch, a couple of recliners, a love seat and a wall mounted television. There was a coffee table with popcorn, soda, chips, and salsa. It looked like the perfect place to watch anything from Saturday morning cartoons to the Superbowl. Somehow the two spaces were contradictory and complementary at the same time.

I was seated on the couch and told to help myself to anything. They pointed out the fridge and minibar and then they left. There were no handcuff put on my wrists, no shackles around my legs, no restraints of any kind held me in place, and yet I felt more of a prisoner here than anywhere else I had been. In a minute, I knew why.

The door opened and Saul walked in. I'm not gay. I never have been attracted to the opposite sex in any shape, form or fashion. I thought the first time I saw Saul that he was almost godlike in appearance. I put that off to being delirious from the beating I was in the middle of getting at the time. In a very real sense he rescued me. Besides, my eyes were at least half swollen shut when he came in. But none of that was true this time and I still thought that he was simply too handsome to be human.

I'm not sure how to describe him. In a sense, he is beyond description. He defies description. I suppose that something like Adonis might be used to begin describing him, but that would only be a beginning and a poor one at that. There are guys who have no body fat on them. They've worked, dieted, sweated, and struggled to remove any vestige of fat from their body. This guy made every one of them look like pigs and gluttons. He not only didn't have any body fat on him, he simply didn't have a place for body fat. It would be the literal square peg in a round hole scenario.

His hair was long, blonde, wavy and flowing like ripples on a lake. It was shiny and clean. There wasn't a single hair out of place. It framed his handsome face perfectly, and especially highlighted eyes that were as blue as the sky and just as spacious. I sound more like I'm describing a prom date or maybe a super model, but this guy was more like some kind of super model for guys. Honestly, he was the kind of guy that could steal your girlfriend or even your wife and you would walk away glad that she found someone that much better than you.

He walked over and I gotta say that part of me just wanted to kneel right there in front of him. I really felt like I wasn't even worthy to be in his presence. I felt like I was somehow subhuman, like I had missed a link or twelve in the evolutionary chain, while this guy had almost evolved being human. He was like homo superior.

And then I remembered Jackee holding a knife to her own throat, desperately trying not to slice her own jugular while her hand in open defiance of her own survival started slicing across her throat. I remembered kids, toddlers, and maybe even some babies in the nursery being used and abused by men and women who didn't have the confidence to have sex with another adult. I remembered what it was like to be a mere teenage age boy and have to deal with a pervert who wanted to abuse me. I was old enough and wise enough to defend myself, but these poor kids were raised in an environment of condoned suffering and abuse. I thought of all the times this jerk had entered my head and scrambled my brain to the point that I didn't know whether I was awake or still dreaming, whether it was Monday or Friday, whether I had spent a day with Jackee or a year. It was all very confusing, and this guy had caused it all.

He extended his hand for a greeting and I did the polite thing and stood to shake his hand, when what I really wanted to do was kick this guy so hard in the groin that he choked on them. But I needed to play it cool for now. I had to buy Joseph and Tye some more time and maybe I could figure out what made this guy tick, besides his own ego of course.

"I am sorry for the problems we've had," he said cordially. Problems? What problems? I woke up to a world where up was down and down was up. It was a place where right was no longer right and there really wasn't any wrong at all. It was a place where the truth was whatever this guy wanted it to be that particular day. And on top of all that, this jerkwad shoved memories in my head that didn't belong and took out information that might have been important. On top of all that, he killed every Christian he got his hands on and my future wife and Uncle in law were now Christians.

"Yeah, so why don't you just let me go and we'll call it even," I suggested.

"I really don't understand you, Mr. Blue," he said, ignoring my suggestion. That was totally rude of him; I suppose he never read Miss Manners. "I have given you everything a man could ask for and yet you rebel. I have given you the world on a silver platter, and you refuse me."

"The world ain't yours to give. I believe God's name is on that deed."

"I don't believe in God."

"And I don't believe in you, yet there you are," I countered. We were still standing, but at this comment, he laughed and sat back in one of the recliners. I took a seat on the couch and threw my feet up on the coffee table.

"Go ahead, Mr. Blue, make yourself at home. After all, I had this office made especially for you. It is to be yours if you cooperate."

"Yeah, well, don't redecorate just yet. I won't be cooperating."

"Again, I simply don't understand. I offer you the love of a beautiful woman, even two beautiful women, and yet you refuse to help me. I made you famous, and still you don't cooperate. I give you money and everything you could possibly want, and yet here we are at odds with one another. I will have your cooperation, one way or another."

"You wanna know why God doesn't give us everything we want? Because we would always want more than he gave us no matter what. And you ain't God." Again he laughed, only this was a sick, humorless laugh, with no mirth at all.

"I will be a god," he declared. "I will go to the heights of heaven, and I will sit upon the throne of God." This time it was my turn to laugh. I laughed and laughed and then I laughed just a little more.

"You have got to be kidding me," I finally managed to get out. "That's what this is all about? I've got news for you, bucko, someone said the same thing a long time ago and it didn't work out too good for him."

"Well maybe if he had the benefit of my genius, he might have succeeded."

"For a genius you ain't too smart, cause I know a couple of things you don't. For starters, I know there's only one God. And the other thing is you ain't him." I know I was supposed to be buying time for Tye and Joseph, but I was about ready to wrap this thing up. For one thing, instead of making me want to kneel, all this guy was doing now was making me want to hurl. I mean, how many other people had tried the whole take over the world thing. And even if they managed, which some of them had, how long can it last for them? Everybody dies. Eventually, this guy would too. Maybe he'd last longer than the others who had come before him, but I doubted it. I think the next thing on God's calendar was the peace treaty with Israel, and that would start the clock ticking.

But there were some things I wanted to know, so I asked, "How did you manage it? I mean how did you get people to turn on Christians so quickly?"

"That?" he said, laughing. "That was simple. First of all, I used all sorts of social media to promote the idea. By doing that, I was able to get several Hollywood celebrities to get on board with it. It was in vogue to bash Christians, and the road from bashing to persecuting is a short one, I can tell you."

This guy was making me angrier, sicker and more disgusted by the moment. But not all of my anger was directed at him. It couldn't be, because he wasn't really the one at fault. Don't get me wrong, he was pretty much evil incarnate. But he was only the focal point of the real problem. There was no way he could have led the people in such a drastic change in direction if they hadn't been willing to be led that way.

"Have you ever heard of convergence?" he asked.

"Yeah," I said. "I think I had some in a French restaurant. It gave me gas." He went on as if I hadn't said anything, and I guess I hadn't really said anything that mattered, but I couldn't help getting in my digs when I could. With this guy talking, I could tell those chances were gonna be few and far between.

"Convergence is when things come together near a single point, either in space or in time. There were several different factors that although seeming unrelated, converged together for this to happen.""

"Do tell," I urged. I learned a lot from watching the old Batman shows and from watching Bond. One of the things villains love to do is talk. And just plain common sense and a sense of human nature will tell you that if you can get them to talk about themselves, they'll talk practically forever.

"The first was the rise of radical Islam. You started to see that in your lifetime. Thanks to the weak response of President Carter, the clerics were emboldened to try more and to engage the youth of their countries, appealing to their pride and heritage. Within decades there was a religious fervor that had reached a fever pitch. They were more than happy to imprison Christians. My only problem there was trying to keep them from killing them."

"But you kill us," I said, associating myself with my fellow Christians on purpose. I could have hidden that fact for just a little longer, but I remembered Jesus telling his followers that if they were ashamed of him, then he would be ashamed of them. I was ready to go at anytime.

"True, and if I didn't have use of you, I'd kill you

right now. But it all comes down to timing, doesn't it?" I didn't know. The only timing I knew about was on my old truck. "If we imprisoned the Christians, then we were only protecting ourselves and more importantly, our children. But by killing them and televising it, they ran the risk of making martyrs of the Christians. We couldn't have them being persecuted. But as it turned out, no one really cared, not even their fellow Christians. They were all too busy going about their lives."

"Okay, so that's one thing. What else was going on?"

"The other thing, as I said, was totally unrelated. It was the rise of the homosexual and hypersexual movements."

"Alright, I know what faggots are, but what the heck is hypersexual?"

"Please, no need for the aggression. Hypersexual is just what it sounds like. It's basically sex at light speed, with no holds barred. People want what they want and the Christians were an impediment to their desires. No one wants to be told no, especially when the reason for doing so is a bunch of antiquated rules from an equally antiquated manuscript."

"So kids are now fair game? You know some rules are there for a reason."

"Only if you want to follow them. What might be

right for you may not be right for me. We each make our own paths in life."

"That's about what Jesus said,' I interjected. "Problem is, most of those roads lead to hell and destruction."

"Look around you, Mr. Blue. In my world everyone gets what they want, when they want, as much as they want. It is heaven on earth."

"Not for the kids you rape. For them it's hell on earth."

"A small price to pay. Besides, they are malleable. They adjust and learn."

"Yeah, they learn to rape the next generation," I yelled.

"That reminds me of the other factor in this equation. The Christians themselves."

"Excuse me," I said.

"Christians were an angry, bitter mob of people. They were constantly complaining about something or someone, hardly exhibiting the love that Jesus spoke of. In the end, most of them looked more like the Pharisees who crucified Jesus than the disciples that followed him. They were ignorant of what the Bible had to say about issue and too complacent and apathetic to do anything about the issues they truly cared about. Why do you think abortion remained legal in a nation that was full of Christians when it was obvious to anyone with half a brain that it was killing children?"

"So you're willing to admit that?" I asked incredulous.

"Why not? It's too late for anyone to stop me now. What do a couple of million of children matter in the long run?" This guy was one cold fish. He could admit to murder, rape, child rape and half a dozen other sins and crimes that would make even the most hardened criminal at least blush and he didn't seem to care one bit. But then again, I don't think what he said would have bothered many people in this world, at least not the world of spoiled children who got what they wanted when they wanted it. I doubt that there was much that would bother them.

"And finally," he started, "we come to you, Mr. Blue. You are the final piece in this puzzle."

"Me?" I asked. "What do I have to do with anything? I'm just a guy who went to sleep in a world that was sane and woke up in a world where the inmates are running the asylum."

"Did you really think your being chosen for the project was coincidence? Or that you were simply chosen because you have no family ties? There were hundreds of candidates who fit that description."

"You're talking like you had something to do with

it. You weren't even alive when I was put in suspended animation."

He leaned forward, staring at me intently and curled his lips into an evil grin.

"Mr. Blue, this conspiracy began long before either of us was alive. It dates back to the time of Christ himself, perhaps before. We have been waiting and planning for such a moment as this since that time. And that time is now. All the pieces are in place."

My head was spinning. I still had no idea what he was talking about, but it was obvious that I was an integral part of the plan, but I still didn't know what the plan entailed or how I was supposed to be a part of it. To be honest, I had just been stalling this guy for time. I didn't expect any real answers and the fact that he gave me plenty of answers kind of concerned me. It meant that in his mind, anyway, this was already a done deal and there was nothing I could do about it. Of course, we'd just have to see about that, but for now I wanted more answers, like what part he wanted me to play.

"Come with me," he said, rising from his seat and beckoning for me to do the same. I felt like a cow being led to slaughter, but I didn't have much of a choice.

He took me from the office, down a long hallway that led to an elevator. In the elevator, he inserted a key and turned it counterclockwise. When he did, panel opened, revealing a second keypad with more numbers. All of them began with the letter B, and went in descending order.

"We have several sublevels in this building. The basement is as far as anyone can go without a key for the elevator." Well, that answered my question without me even asking it. He was getting way to good at doing that. It was like he knew in advance what I was gonna say. I just wanted to know who gave him a copy of the script for this comedy and where did I get my copy to study?

We went down to level B9. The elevator doors opened and I felt a blast of cool air. In fact, it was cold enough down here for what we would call hog killing weather. There were row upon row of computer banks, lit from above by fluorescent lighting. He led the way between one of the rows, taking me to a door on the far wall. He inserted another key, pulled out a magnetic card and swiped it across a screen and then put his thumb on a screen for fingerprint scan. The door opened with a slight hiss of air.

"This is CARL," he said with a sweeping motion of his hand. Before me was a giant of a man. He was at least seven, maybe eight foot tall. He was as broad as a barn, with a slim waist. His legs and arms were as big as tree trunks with thick corded muscles. And where Saul was handsome, this guy was almost too good looking to look at. I can honestly say that it was almost painful to look at him. Carl just stood there, eyes closed, still as death. I wondered for a minute if he was dead. I mean, I enjoy a good nap now and then, but I don't usually do it standing up, in a locked room, and with other people looking at me like I'm some kind of museum exhibit.

"Is he real?" I finally managed.

"Yes, he is real, but not quite human; more than human. He is the next link in the evolutionary chain. He is the perfect combination of man and machine, a robot with synthetic flesh, a processor that works like the human brain, only faster and with a memory storage and retrieval system that is unrivaled."

"So if you got him, what do you need me for?" I asked.

"CARL is focal point of this entire computer network," he started. "He is integrated into every program here, as well as all of the minds of everyone above us."

"You mean everyone who has the new body your nanobots provide?" I asked. "Don't they also integrate themselves into the hosts nervous systems and act as a transceiver for CARL so that he can download their memories and upload a whole new reality for each of them, one based on whatever lie you want to tell that day?"

"Simply put, but true," he admitted. "And he can also create temporary realities for the others also, those who don't have the nanobots." Now we were getting somewhere. He said temporary, as if the realities he created would have fallen apart anyway, even without Joseph's intervention. But then hadn't Joseph said as much also? He said that I was in danger if I stayed there. Not because I would accept that reality, but because in accepting that reality, I would also accept the nanobots, thereby inviting Saul and CARL to penetrate my mind at will. I would have subjected myself to them, as Jackee said. She couldn't surrender her will to God, no matter how much she wanted to, because she had already sold her soul to this monstrosity.

"Once again, where do I come in?" I asked impatiently.

"CARL is the almost the final stage of Artificial Intelligence. He can think, reason, and even simulate some emotions, although not well. But what he can't do is dream. Dreams are born out of the angst, worry, fears and frustrations of the day, but CARL knows none of those things."

"What's so important about dreaming?" I asked. I thought it was highly overrated myself, since I had done about forty years worth of it recently.

"Because those in a dream state can be reached on a subconscious level much easier and deeper than those on a conscious level. There we can penetrate the psyche of every human being on the planet. Once we have them, between CARL's automated systems and the billions of human minds we'll have at our disposal, we can actually alter reality. Do you understand? We can become gods!" He screamed that last part with the fervor of a man who has begun to believe his own press. This guy was definitely in need of a good tailor who could make him a real tight suit with lots of belts and a real estate agent who could set him up in an apartment with padded walls.

"Yeah," I said. "I understand you're a fruitcake. You can't change reality. God is the only one who can create. We only get to alter what already has been created."

"But that was the promise of the beginning," he said with a religious zeal. "We were promised that we would be like gods, and CARL and I are going to have that power with your help, Mr. Blue. You will integrate your subconscious with that of CARL and then you will use your ability to lucid dream. With your talent, and CARL's processing ability, you will be able to change the thought patterns of millions of people each night, so that they will willingly accept my nanobot transformation and will become totally subservient to me. Once I have such an army, I can challenge the gates of Heaven itself."

"You are looney,"

"Am I? Think of it, Mr. Blue. When the people united at the tower of Babel, God was forced to act.

He confounded their language because he knew a united mankind could challenge him. We will be one. We will act as one. We will think as one."

"One problem, chief, I ain't gonna do it. I won't willingly accept the nanobots, so you can't force me to do anything for you. You can try torture, which I'm sure you will, but I still won't grant your wish." I wasn't being overconfident or cocky. I knew my limits and I also knew the limits of my morality, and this went way past anything I would do willingly. I knew I would die before caving in to his demands, and death would be a welcome relief.

"Do you know what happens to those who receive the nanobots, but are unwilling to cooperate?" he asked. I didn't know, I didn't want to know, but I did know he was going to tell me anyway, so I decided to flow with it.

"Do tell," I said.

"The nanobots force their way into the neural pathways of the brain, causing irreparable brain damage. The invasion causes the brain to react in such a way that the patient hallucinates with unspeakable horrors. Finally, the brain hemorrhage, causing the brain to swell to such a point that it will actually crack the skull from the inside out. I've seen it and it's not a pretty picture."

"I can live with that." I guess I actually couldn't, but that was his point, wasn't it? Maybe I couldn't live with it, but I wouldn't mind dying with it. If God chose to save me, great, but if wanted to let me die a painful death, I'd deal with that as it came. I was readyo go. I'd miss Tye, or maybe she'd miss me, but I'd be with Jesus and out of this crazy world.

"Look at the monitor behind you," he ordered. I complied with his order and looked. What I saw turned my stomach. Joseph was on his knees, head bent over and a man with a sword or scimitar was standing over him, poised to strike. Saul pressed a button and a small microphone appeared out of the wall.

"Are you comfortable, Joseph?" he asked politely.

"Fine, thank you," Joseph responded coolly. I don't think it was the response Saul expected. It seemed to shake him a little.

"Let him go," I demanded.

"Gladly," Saul responded. "Just do as I ask, and he will be freed."

"Whatever it is, don't do it," Joseph yelled. "I would rather be a door keeper in the house of God than serve in the palaces of man." I don't know if Joseph knew for sure I was listening, or just guessed at Saul's intent. But there was a deeper question probing at my mind. If Joseph was here, then where was Tye? The thought of this monster hurting her was almost more than I could bear.

"Do I have your cooperation?" he asked. What could I do? I was caught between the literal rock and a hard place. If I didn't work with him, then Joseph would die, but if I did work with him, millions of souls would lose their opportunity for salvation. I thought about Jackee, wanting to pray, but being unable to do so. She would have accepted Jesus if she could have. I honestly believed that, but because she had given herself over to Saul for the thirty pieces of silver of having a great body and an extended life, that opportunity was gone forever. How would it be for those who were fooled into doing the same thing? Would they have a chance to accept Jesus? Did they now? They had rejected him over and over, so did they still have a chance. I couldn't make that decision for them, even if it meant Joseph's life. I was helpless, and Saul knew it.

"Do it," he ordered. The blade came down swiftly and cut clean thru. It was the only consolation I could have, that and the fact that I saw what looked like a smile on Joseph's face as the blade went thru. Now the question was could I do the same if it was Tye out there? Would I be able to have the strength needed? I could stand my own death, and I had just proven I could watch a good friend die, but could I watch the woman I loved die? I had given in to Saul earlier when he threatened Jackee, and the stakes weren't as high then. I almost expected him to bring out Jackee next.

Saul pressed a button on the console in front of him and the screen went blank. Then he pressed another button and two goons came in, grabbed me harshly and put handcuffs on me behind my back.

"Prepare him for the procedure," he commanded.

"I thought it wouldn't work," I commented. "You're wasting your time."

"Perhaps, but then either way, my bases are covered. If you don't work out, my plans are only delayed, not thwarted. And, oh, by the way, thank you for bringing me the girl."

"What are you talking about?" I demanded.

"Joseph's niece, Tye. I've been looking for a virgin of Jewish descent for some time. As you can imagine, virgin's are a rare commodity in our world, and to find one of Jewish descent is even rarer."

"I still don't understand," I said, struggling against the goons holding me. A nod from Saul and they unhanded me.

"As I said, my plans may be delayed, but they will come to pass. If you fail to cooperate, then when Tye has the baby I've planted in her, it will serve the same purpose, a true integration between man and machine. CARL will have a son, and your precious Tye will be the vassal for his entrance into the world. The first child born of a virgin was the Son of God.

Who do you think will claim this child?" It was all I could do not to rush him. I knew I probably wouldn't make it, but I was certainly going to try. But before I did, I needed to throw him off guard. Right now, he'd expect my anger to get the best of me, and with my hands behind my back, a simple sidestep on his part would introduce my head to the wall.

"You think of yourself as some kind of new god, but you're just another one of Satan's puppets, like Herod, Pilate, Caesar, and Hitler. Once he has what he wants, which is that baby, you'll be yesterday's garbage, ready to be thrown to the curb."

"Perhaps, perhaps not. But you won't be here to find out." It was now or never. I ducked my head down, took one giant step, and then leaped forward as hard as I could, thrusting the top of my head towards his way too perfect nose. If I had my way it wouldn't be perfect for long. I was satisfied to feel a tremendous pain on the top of my skull at the same as I heard a sickening crunching sound that I assumed was his nose. I assumed it was his nose because I also heard a scream of agonizing pain from Saul. It was probably the first time and last time on earth he felt pain. He better get used to it, because when he died, he would feel plenty of it for a lifetime.

"Get him out of here!" he screamed in fury. Score one for the little guys. Of course, the score was Saul about a thousand and me only one, but God was on my side and no matter what the score was here, in

Heaven I'd still win.

CHAPTER TWELVE

I was strapped completely naked to a hospital table. These guys and gals had a real problem with the human body and the tremendous amount of skin they wanted displayed. Although, come to think of it, hospital gowns didn't do that much for covering skin either. Straps were placed across my chest and abdomen. My legs were tied down to the sides of the raised rails, as well as my arms. Whatever happened at this point was beyond my capability to change. All I could do is lie here helpless and wonder what kind of pain and fear Tye was feeling. I couldn't imagine what must be going through her mind. The poor kid was barely out of her teens and might very well be carrying what would be the Anti-Christ. At the very best, she was carrying some kind of almost alien life form in her womb, a hybrid between man and machine. It was funny, now that I thought about it. Saul accused Christians of being from a different planet. He accused them of having an alien entity inside of them, and yet he was the one putting a form of a alien, or at the very least foreign, seed in each one of his people.

I felt a pain stabbing into my right arm. Turning my head slightly, which is all I could do, I saw a woman putting an IV into my arm. Was it Jackee? I wondered if she was still alive. Saul had promised that he'd let her live, but then he was a baby rapist, serial murderer, thief, and self-proclaimed god, so why not a liar as well. Not that I was judging, mind you. I just called them as I saw them. And I wasn't going to see much of anything in just a minute. A mask went over my face. I assumed it was some kind of gaseous anesthesia and I tried to hold my breath against it, but it was no use. Besides, even if I could hold my breath forever, I couldn't stay awake forever. And I figured the real damage was coming in the steady drip, drip of the IV as it flowed into my veins, arteries and capillaries. Slowly, but surely, I was being invaded by a foreign entity. Soon I would be like one of those pod people on that old science fiction movie. Even then, as if it were some sort of prophecy, the only way to fight them off was to stay awake. And I couldn't do that much longer.

It may have been the gas or it may have been just sheer exhaustion, but either way I felt myself begin to drift off to sleep. I was going to fight it as long as I could, but I felt like a ninety eight pound weakling in the ring with Ali. Okay, if I couldn't fight sleep, maybe I could run from it. No, it was no good. My mind was beginning to fog. I felt myself drift into sleep, shook myself awake. Drift, shake. It became a repeated pattern for the next several minutes. Was that all? How about for the next several hours? Or even days? But no, I would be asleep soon and I couldn't stop it.

Two thoughts penetrated through the fog and mist of oncoming unconsciousness. The first thought I had wasn't so much a thought as a one way conversation. I prayed over and over to God to watch over Tye and keep her safe. I prayed for Jackee too. I know she said there was no way to overcome the obstacle of Saul's invasion of her soul, but then God did that which no one else could. He was God, after all, and didn't let things like that stop him. Or did he? I struggled with that. It might be that Jackee had taken a form of the mark of the beast. I know the tribulation hadn't started proper just yet, but it seemed to me that there were some of the players were moving into position and that some of the conditions for the tribulation were already in effect. I knew there were several series of sevens. Seven seals followed by seven bowls or something like that. Seven followed by seven. God's number of completeness, meaning judgment would be swift, harsh and complete. And Jackee might very well fall under that judgment.

At least Joseph had escaped. I thought of it that way. He had escaped the coming period of God's wrath and Satan's final war against God's people. He was in Heaven now, having his tears wiped away and receiving, I supposed, the rewards earned for his time here. I guess one of them would be a martyrs crown, if there was such a thing. If there wasn't then there ought to be. He deserved....

Face it, he deserved hell, just like the rest of us. We all do. We compare ourselves to each other and think we're doing pretty doggone good. I ain't Hitler, after all. I don't deal drugs to little kids or rape and

molest little girls and boys. So I'm a good guy, right.
Not hardly. First of all, just cause I don't doesn't mean
I ain't capable. I could be the next Hitler, Mussolini,
or Marx. It was all about grace freely given and
nothing about me earning anything.

My second thought was on what was going to
happen next. Saul wanted me to enter the dreamworld
while connected to CARL, whatever that acronym
stood for. While I was in the Army, which I
technically I guess I still was. I wonder who I should
see about back pay. Here I am wondering about back
pay when a maniac wants me to have my brainwaves
integrated with CARL's so that between the two of us,
we might alter reality. Well, so be it. If I was going to
teach CARL something, then it was going to be a
lesson he wouldn't soon forget and one that Saul
would learn as well. If I had the chance to alter
reality, then I had the chance to alter it in my favor for
a change.

I allowed myself to drift off to sleep, but only
after setting a few parameters for myself. I wanted to
be in a flat field of grass when I woke in my dream.
Yeah, that sounds kind of like an oxymoron, but that's
how it works for me. I go to sleep in this reality, and I
awaken in a reality I've created for myself. Sometimes
I'll create a whole world. No, literally a whole world,
something I can travel and explore. I'll seek out
mysteries that I placed there, only to hide them from
myself in a further subconscious lever. It gets pretty
freaky sometimes and there are times when I've fooled

myself into believing I was awake when I was still sound asleep. The hardest part is maintaining the illusion of your dreamscape. I called it that because I remembered reading a book by that title when I was just ten or eleven. It scared the heebie-jeebies out of me. It also started me on the path to lucid dreaming.

The problem to maintaining your dreamscape is that it requires a tremendous amount of focus while your mind is also creating the realities of people, circumstances, and other objects that might come in handy, like a hammer if you want to be a carpenter or a scalpel if you want to be a surgeon. The picture I'm painting is probably about as clear as mud, but unless you've experienced it for yourself, there's just no good way to describe it for someone else.

Suddenly, the earth I created began to rumble beneath my feet and began to crack in great chasms. It wasn't me doing this and I hadn't lost concentration, so I could only assume I had company, and that he was angry, or at least a bit peeved. The earth spread further and further apart, making me concentrate to hold my balance. I thought about firm footing underneath me and the grass became concrete. The concrete flowed away from me like grey lava, filling in the chasms and creating a vast parking lot in every direction.

On the horizon stood a man. Judging from the distance and his comparative height, I was pretty sure I was looking at CARL. He was coming my way, but he wasn't in any hurry. I thought of a couch and took a seat on the soft leather. The sun was high in the sky, casting no shadows. It was just a little too bright, so I brought in some clouds to tone down the brightness. The early days of my experimenting with lucid dreaming were intoxicating, and this was reminding me why. I could do or become just about anything I could imagine. Did I say just about anything? If I could imagine it, then I could be it. If I could dream it, it became a reality, at least here. It may not have had any substance compared to the outside world, but then again, neither did the outside world when compared to heaven. The real world wasn't the one we saw every day. That was just as much a shadow compared to the life beyond death as this was to my waking hours.

I wish the big jerk would hurry up. I wasn't exactly in a hurry to face him, but I didn't really feel like dragging this out either. Just for fun, I had a big, black, stretch limousine pull up alongside him. A chauffeur got out, ran around to the back door and helped CARL into the fancy car before shutting the door and returning to the driver's seat. With luck, they would be here in less than a minute now. There are times when I'm not a patient man and there are other times when I'm a very impatient man. There is a difference.

The car pulled up in front of me. Again, the chauffeur hopped out, opened the door, this time allowing CARL to depart the vehicle, and then went back to the driver's seat and drove off.

"Have a seat," I said and produced an overstuffed and oversized recliner.

"Show me how you do this," he said, taking a seat and crossing his legs.

"Sorry, but a good magician never reveals his secrets," I replied. Besides, I don't understand all that I know about what I do. I'd like to say I've got it all together, but not only do I NOT have it all together; I can hardly remember where I put all the pieces.

He rose to his feet and began to approach me. If he meant to get physical, it was a mistake on his part. In the other world, he could kick my tail six ways from Sunday, which was an expression I didn't get but used a lot anyways. I stood also, bracing myself for an attack that never came.

"I must be able to produce these things for myself."

"You were doing pretty good with that earthquake, "I said.

"That was only a reflection of the way that I felt. I felt out of place, as if my world were breaking apart. So when I entered this world, my new world began to shake and tremble, coming apart beneath me." I almost felt sorry for the big guy. In a sense, at least here, he wasn't much more than a child, a sort of big baby. I said I almost felt sorry for him. He was still one half of the disastrous due that was trying to enslave humanity, take over the world, and challenge God. He was not one of my favorite people. I had already scratched him off my Christmas card mailing list.

"So you were just being a big crybaby?" I asked. Hey, subtlety ain't my strong suit. Neither is being polite, friendly, or just plain nice. A lot of kids get the whole, "doesn't play well with others" note attached to their report kids at some point in their lives. My report card had a note that said, "Should be segregated from society." And, I guess, in a way I was.

The sky grew dark and ominous. The sun disappeared entirely behind a bank of swirling, dark clouds. Lightning flashed from cloud to cloud, building energy up in them before finally exploding with lightning across the sky and down to the ground, throwing up great chunks of concrete when it hit.

"I'm not a baby," he screamed. Yeah, and that little hissy fit you just through is just the thing you need to do to prove how mature you are. I suspected that CARL wasn't much more than a child mentally after his admission of being fearful upon entering this world, but his fit and subsequent declaration only sealed the deal. Now my entire strategy had to change. I had planned to crush this guy under a mountain of imaginary rocks, but I could hardly do that now. I still had to defeat him, but in a different way.

"Yeah, I can see that." There was a shift in the

atmosphere. It was subtle and if I hadn't been using a portion of my concentration to maintain the environment we were in, I probably wouldn't have noticed it. But the change in CARL was a whole lot more noticeable. He straightened his posture. The tears that threatened to escape the corners of his eyes suddenly dried up. His whole demeanor changed.

"That was only one aspect of my personality," he said. "Having assimilated thousands upon thousands of men, women, and children, sometimes in stressful situations it's difficult to maintain the proper personality. I apologize for my less than mature behavior. It won't happen again. Now please explain how you conjure this world in which we inhabit. How do you maintain its sophistication and proper aura?"

"Not telling," I said, adopting the same tone as the younger CARL. "And you can't make me."

"We'll see about that," CARL threatened. "I can't make worlds with the sophistication you can. Not yet, anyway. But I can control time here. For instance, I can transport us, in essence, to forty days into the future." I felt like my heart was racing away with itself. Then it was racing with my mind and unfortunately neither of them was winning. My lungs felt as if they were on fire. And then came the hunger and thirst. I was dehydrating in a matter of moments and starving to death at the same time. I called out to God for help. In spite of being able to create worlds within my imagination, or maybe because of it, I recognized my total dependence on God through his Son, Jesus Christ. He entered our dreamworld of rules and regulations to show us how to navigate through these treacherous waters. Most of us, most of the time, still managed to crash our ships into the rocks along the coast, but he also came to forgive us for all of those things if we just accepted his help and forgiveness. I needed him now more than ever before. No, that wasn't right. I had always needed him with the same desperation, this only revealed it to me.

"Take your best shot," I said defiantly. Maybe it wasn't the smartest thing to say, but it was the first thing to pop into my brain, so I went with it.

"Here, Mr. Blue," he said, sounding much like his father, Saul. "You must be hungry. It has been forty long days since your last meal. Take some of these concrete chunks and turn them into bread for yourself. Or maybe a cake or a pie, just whatever you like."

Here's the thing, I should have been hungry. I should have been starving and ready to eat my own shoe without even a drop of ketchup. And the way my feet smelled, I would have had to be pretty doggone hungry to even think about eating one of those. And just how long could a body go without water? I know we were in a dream state, but in this particular type of dream state, the world we were in was a close reflection of reality, but I wasn't even thirsty. My mouth wasn't dry. My throat wasn't sore or parched. I was just fine in every respect. I could have whipped up not just some hot cross buns or some yummy yeast rolls, but a seven course meal complete with appetizer and dessert. It would have been easy, but the thing was, I didn't need to. I didn't want to. And I wasn't going to.

"I'll pass," I said. It didn't seem to make him very happy, but I noticed he held his temper. There were no earthquakes or great chasms forming in the ground beneath our feet. He was learning to control his temper. Kudos for him, but I still wasn't going to play his game.

There was another shimmer rippling through the sky overhead. It reminded me of those old shows where someone is having a flashback. Just before the flashback begins, there are some wavy lines that appear to let everyone know that a flashback is coming. For me, the ripple let me know a personality change was coming. I could expect a new aspect to an old foe.

"Mr. Blue," he said congenially, "there's no need for us to be enemies."

"I agree," I said. "Just let me and Tye go free and you'll never have to worry about me coming back. We'll walk out and never even look back, like Lot leaving Sodom."

"I was hoping we could come to some sort of agreement. I know you don't like the deplorable moral conditions of our society. Together we could do something about that."

There was something compelling about his voice. It was almost mesmerizing. I saw myself as the boy in the tree with that big snake in the Jungle Book. If I listened too much longer, I might actually come around to this guys way of thinking, and if I wasn't careful, I'd end up in the belly of this beast, and I didn't have a big talking bear around to save my sorry hide. Where were all the good animated characters when you needed them?

"What are you saying? You're the one who set up the system where it's perfectly fine for people to rape young children. Having second thoughts?"

"I tried to give the people what they wanted. I wanted them to be happy, to be fulfilled. Is that so wrong?"

"Raping children is wrong."

"Of course. We need a moral compass. And that's where you come in, Mr. Blue. If you join with me, we can guide these people to become better. We can set up a system of rules to follow, with just punishments for those who violate the rules. It will be a just and fair system. But I need your help. You need to become one with me so that we can implement these new rules through their dreams."

It sounded too good to be true. And there was a great reason for that. It was too good to be true. First of all, I wasn't about to become one with such an evil creature as this. Second, I would have to turn my back on God and declare either this miscreant or myself as god, which wasn't about to happen. God was the creator and he was the only one who could decide right from wrong. Man had to set up rules and regulations for a civilized society to grow, but even then everyone still had the free will to rebel against those rules. Even God, who could do what he wanted, backed down for whatever reason when it came to the absence of free will.

"No, thanks," I stated.

"What do you mean?" he asked.

"I thought you were a genius. I used small words so you would understand, but I'll explain it anyway. No is a negative response to your request. It means uh-uh, not gonna happen, forget about it. And thanks means I was just being polite, cause Miss Martha didn't like it much when I was rude."

The sky was darkening. The white fluffy clouds of a few minutes ago ran away from the dark, ominous growth that was now blocking out the sun. He was still controlling his temperature somewhat, but the pot of his anger had been put on the stove and was simmering pretty good. Another few minutes and another couple of jabs and he'd blow completely. I probably didn't want to be around when that happened, but at least for now it didn't look like I had much of a choice.

The strain was also taking a toll on me. I wasn't sure how much longer I could handle his onslaught of charisma and charm. He really was hypnotizing to listen to. Zeke used to tell me that to prepare for times like these, I should have scripture memorized to use. I really wish I had listened to Zeke more. It seems that the older I get, the wiser him and Miss Martha turned out to be.

The best I could do was think about characters of the Bible, a lot of them had gone through either things like this or even worse things. Joseph had been sold by his brothers into slavery, accused of rape, and forgotten by his supposed friend. And I thought I was having a bad couple of days. By the end of the story, he's second to Pharaoh in power and able to put his brothers in their place, but he doesn't. Instead, he tells them they meant it for evil, but God meant it for good.

I thought about Miss Martha and Zeke. It would have been nice to be raised by them, but God had a different plan in mind. It would have been nice for them to make it home after seeing me graduate, but God and a drunk driver had different plans. I didn't blame God anymore. I did for a long time, but I just realized that Joseph's God was my God, and that He allowed bad stuff to happen to me, but it all turned out good in the end. God was still large and in charge, so there wasn't gonna be anything I had to worry about.

"Come with me, Mr. Blue. I want to show you something." He walked off into the horizon. I thought about turning around and heading in the opposite direction, but I didn't have any place to go anyway. Without warning, the ground in front of me convulsed and rose. It went higher and higher and all I could do was just hang on. CARL didn't seem to be having any problem. He just stood there, stoic, calm and collected. Of course it helped that he was the one who caused the rift in the first place.

I thought about all that he had done. He had a limit that was for sure. I could do just about anything here I wanted to. The dream was a blank canvas and I was DaVinci. I could paint the most beautiful masterpiece, or have an abstract world of various shapes and sizes. The choice was completely mine. I could create beauty and elegance or just have a plain jane, run as you want

CARL, on the other hand, only influenced our environment with negative emotions like anger, fear, and worry. He assimilated people beneath him, absorbing their information, knowledge, and personality. But beneath the placid surface of their existence, they felt the same emotions that seemed to drive CARL's visions. It was no wonder that his personality was so dark, since the hearts of those he absorbed were dark with sin and worry about that sin. Even in their stupor of sex, drugs and alcohol, something just below the surface told them that one day it would all end and that the bill would be due, payment paid in full. CARL was the product of his own darkness.

He led me into an office type structure. On the wall were hundreds, perhaps thousands of monitors. They seemed to go on in every direction for as far as the eye could see. Beneath each of them was a placard, designating the city where the image originated from. There was Paris, Hong Kong, London, Moscow, along with other large European and Asian cities. Some of the monitors had signs from cities and towns that I didn't recognize. The images they had were of small towns and villages. As I looked more, I saw cities such as New York, Pittsburgh, Miami and Seattle, every major metropolis. Alongside them were towns of less than a hundred. Every sort of city was represented, from small rural towns to major metropolitan cities.

"Follow me and all of this will be yours to control," CARL whispered in my ear. "All of it at your disposal. These people are mine and I am theirs. I have fulfilled the command of my creator."

"What wish is that?" I asked foolishly.

"For all to be one. I am one with them and they are one with me. As my creator and I are one, so they are one with me and our creator," he said with a sweep of his hand down row after row of monitors. "And you could be one with us, to control all. To insure order and tranquility. Do not turn us down so quickly, Mr. Blue. I know the power you have."

"And what power is that?" I asked.

"The power to control. You controlled Jackee. I witnessed it myself."

"I never controlled Jackee. All I ever wanted her to have was the opportunity to have a choice to accept Jesus, and you took that from her."

"That's where you are mistaken, Mr. Blue. I gave her that chance before I killed her." His words stunned me. Jackee was alive. He had promised to keep her alive. It made no sense to kill her, but then there was little in this world that made sense. "I wanted to test her, so I released my hold on her after you left. Almost immediately she fell to her knees and started calling out to your Jesus. It was sickening me, so I took over control again and had her slice her own throat. Her last words were 'Forgive me'. That kind of power and influence must be mine. Become one with me."

I had taken too much. This creep brags about killing an innocent woman as if he were just putting down a rabid dog and then asks me to become one with such insanity. I had held me peace for as long as I could, but every man has his limits and I was way past mine.

"How about you let your lips become one with my....." I never had the chance to finish the sentence. I guess maybe I got on his bad side, because the next thing I knew, I was thrust upwards as the ground beneath me shook in gigantic waves. It was like surfing, only there was no water, just mounds and mounds of dirt, grass and debris cascading over and over in an endless tidal wave of destruction. Eventually, the waves coalesced into one gigantic tsunami that towered over everything else. It was there that I found myself, standing on the edge of a dangerous precipice.

"I had thought to allow you the choice to jump, but I think not," he said and pushed me over the edge. I heard him say, just as I fell, "Save yourself or die."

I could have saved myself. There were thousands of times during my long sleep that I had conjured similar scenarios. It was kind of a thrill to place yourself into dangerous situations, only to find a last minute solution. There used to be a theory that if you died in your sleep, then you would die physically as well. It's why people often dream about falling, but never of hitting the bottom below them. I always wondered how they tested that theory. Was there any way to know for sure if dream death caused physical death? Well, it was just too bad that there weren't any psychologists around to record this phenomenon for posterity because I wasn't gonna give this joker the satisfaction of saving myself. I had placed myself into God's care and either he would save me and allow me just a little more time on this earth, hopefully with Tye by my side, or I'd end up in Heaven, reunited with Zeke, Miss Martha, and hopefully Jackee. I hoped that by releasing her for that little bit of time, Saul/CARL had allowed her the chance for salvation unwittingly. She had asked for forgiveness, and wasn't that all anyone had to do? After all, the thief on the cross had just asked to be remembered, and Jesus told him they'd be in paradise together that day.

Knowing this was my last fall, I decided to enjoy it. I could have screamed. I could have panicked. I could have tried flapping my arms like a duck. There were lots of things I could have done, but the one thing I did do was trust God. Live or die, it was totally in his hands and either way, I'd be totally out of the hands of that lunatic above me.

The fall seemed to last forever, but this wasn't actual time. This was dream time, and our perception of time in dreams changes. It's why people can dream of a whole day or of even a week in just a few minutes of sleep. I fell and fell, gaining speed until I reached terminal velocity. I was never good in physics, so I'm not sure what the terminal velocity of a two hundred pound man is, but I can know it was pretty darned quick. I was a speeding bullet heading for the target just below me.

Then, without warning, there was no below me. There was no above me. I was still falling, but now I felt like I was falling to my right. A little more time passed and I began falling to my left. Then I was actually falling upwards again, regaining ground I had lost. It was a roller coaster ride without the benefit of a seatbelt, tracks, or even a cart to ride in, but man I was sure enjoying the ride. I closed my eyes and let the ride take me wherever it wanted.

I felt a jolt. I guess that was the bottom. I should be dead, but I didn't feel dead. Just out of curiosity, I opened my eyes. There in front of me was the same grassy plain I had envisioned at the beginning of the dream. But this plain was slightly different. I couldn't quite put my finger on it, but I think the difference was that it really existed. This was no dream. I was in a grassy field somewhere. But anywhere was better than where I just left. I was so astonished at my surroundings that at first I didn't realize there was a hand squeezing mine.

"Hey stranger," she said softly.

It was Tye. Maybe I was wrong and I did die, cause her smile made me feel like I was in Heaven.

CHAPTER THIRTEEN

I turned to her and held her. I kissed her over and over and over again. I simply couldn't get enough of her. I wanted to hold her endlessly and never ever let her go again.

"Blue, we have a problem," she said between kisses.

"Ya think?" I asked. I could think of a multitude of problems, starting with I didn't know where we were, how we got there, or who else knew where we were. But those problems paled in comparison to the sheer pleasure of holding the one person you love, the one you would gladly give your life for. If two people are fortunate enough to have that kind of love and any time at all together, then they are rich beyond measure. I just wanted to increase our wealth by finding out how we could get as far away from Saul as I could.

"Blue, I'm serious. I'm pregnant. I think I'm about three months along, according to what I overheard. And, Blue, the baby isn't yours."

"Yes it is," I said nonchalantly.

"No, I think I would have remembered that. Besides, we haven't known each other three months. And we haven't known each other at all that way, "she declared.

"Doesn't matter," I stated and I meant it. Now I just needed her to understand. "You are mine and I am yours, if you'll have me." She assured me that of course I was hers and that she was mine. It made me feel like a little schoolboy passing notes between classes asking if she liked me and would she please check yes or no. Please, oh please, let her mark yes. And, she did, much to my relief and utter satisfaction. "It doesn't matter because you are mine, the baby is inside of you, and I can't have one without the other. We'll get married, raise our child, and live as well as we can for as long as we can."

"You make it sound easy," she said.

"Nothing's easy, but it is settled. It is what it is

and we just have to deal with whatever God hands us. Zeke taught me that." She seemed to accept that, and I was really glad, because now we had to make some tough decisions and this was her land more than my land. It was also more her time than my time. She might have some insight on where we were.

"There used to be an agricultural substation north of town," she offered. "It might have this kind of grass for the livestock they were raising."

"What happened?" I asked.

"Some militant vegetarians thought it was inhumane to keep the cows in a prison like this." I looked around. I didn't see any fences, but if this had been a substation like she suspected the fences were there, but they must have been a long ways off, which meant this was one big prison. "So they forced the authorities to herd the cows outside of the fence so that the cows could be free to roam."

"What happened?" I wanted to know, although I already suspected.

"The cows stood just outside the fence and slowly starved to death. The farmers working here all left when the cows did, so no one was here to intervene."

"And once again, well intentioned people screw up things for everyone else. Did you know the word vegetarian comes from an Indian word that means, 'can't hunt'."

She laughed and so did I. It was good to have the time to enjoy her company, but we really had to make a decision of some kind. I thought about the people in the Old Testament. For them it was kinda easy. God was there to lead them by the hand, and sometimes had to actually had to take them by the hand to get them to move. God led the Jews after they left Egypt by a pillar of fire at night and a cloud by the day. They moved when he moved and stopped when He stopped. Pretty simple.

Then the prophets told the people what to do. It was a little more complicated because they had to find a prophet, but it still worked out pretty good when they actually listened to the prophets. Then the New Testament Apostles had the Holy Spirit poured out on them. And every once in a while, Jesus still showed up, like he did for the Apostle Paul.

I used to ask Zeke how to feel the leadership and direction of God. If there was anyone I knew of that felt God's leading hand, it was Zeke, and Miss Martha, of course. Most of the people in our area were still on party lines when it came to phones in the home. Everyone got to listen in on everyone else's calls, especially the old gossips and busybodies. Miss Martha, however, had a private line that went right to God's office. I was sure of that. She didn't even have to go through his secretary.

The last time I asked Zeke was at my Basic Training graduation. I was thinking about going to

Airborne training, but it would stop me from going overseas, and I didn't know what to do.

"Son," Zeke answered, "the Bible only promises to be a light to our feet. Do you know why that is?" I didn't, naturally.

"No," I answered honestly.

"Cuz all it will do is light the next step. When you take that, then God will light another step for you. Take that and another step is lit. Pretty soon, putting one foot in front of the other, you're walking the path God laid out for you."

"How'd you get to be so smart, old man?" I asked tenderly.

"Same way as everybody else," he said, "I just mess up a lot and try to learn from my mistakes." By this time, Miss Martha, who had been talking with some of the other ladies, joined us.

"If messing up makes you smart," she joked, "then the two of you should be geniuses."

"Mom, Dad, I love you. Thank you for all you've done for me." We hugged then. It was our last hug before a drunk driver sent them to Heaven. It was the first time since I had been taken from their, no, I mean, our, home that I had called them Mom and Dad. As it turned out, it was also the last time.

I turned back to Tye. She was completely lost out

here. She could fare for herself in the city, probably better than me. This was my forte. I was more in my element here than I had been the whole time since I woke up. That made me think of Jackee. I sure did hope she was in Heaven.

"I guess if the city is south of us, then we ought to go north. That will put the greatest distance between us and the loonies who run this place. It looks to me like God has given us a pretty good opportunity to make like a banana and split, so let's not disappoint him." Normally I would have made an inventory of our assets and counted out the deficits that faced us, but we were completely void of any assets other than what was on us, which wasn't much. Our best bet was just to start moving and hope for the best. I set up a rudimentary compass using a stick to mark the rotation of the sun. That gave us a basic understanding of which way north was, so that's where we went.

Along the way, I kept my eyes peeled for hidden treasures. The things people threw away could become a survival kit for anyone in the wild. We weren't exactly in the wild, but we didn't have anything to help us survive out here either. If it rained, we had no shelter. And, if it rained we had no way to gather water, which was going to be an important factor. It wasn't tremendously hot, but Tye was carrying a three month old baby and I had just come out of a dream reality where I had fasted for forty days. That didn't affect my real body, but it did a number on my mind. I thought I was absolutely starving. I noticed an old log and kicked it over. There were a number of beetles there and I grabbed a couple.

They were crunchy, slimy, juicy, bitter, and totally gross, but absolutely the best thing I had ever eaten.

"Want some," I offered Tye. For some reason she declined. Girls can be like that. I, on the other hand, was hungry and willing to eat whatever came my way, whether bug or steak, although I'd choose the steak given the option.

We had walked for a couple of hours when I spotted something shiny on the side of the road. It was a butter knife! Yeah, most of the time people don't get that excited about silverware, but I was willing to take whatever I could get. I also found an old bicycle inner tube. Luckily for me, it was cast under an old log and hadn't got much sun, so it wasn't dry rotted. While I was digging it out, I found two more useful things, an old tin can and a two liter soda bottle. With some bailing wire and an old gum wrapper, I could make a nuclear bomb and the rocket to launch it. I'm just kidding. No one could be that good.

Picking up the bottle, I spotted a hard flat stone, which was just the perfect thing I needed to sharpen the butter knife. It would be slow work, but I could do it while we were walking and we had nothing but time on our hands. It was slow going, and neither one of us were very talkative at the moment. Tye had a lot of bad stuff on her plate that she needed to work through in her own time. There was the death of Joseph. That sick psycho Saul had made her watch the execution as well. She said she didn't blame me, and I think for the most part she didn't, but I also think there was a part of her that thought I should have done more. I know there was a big part of me that thought I should have done more.

By the time the sun was setting low, I had a pretty good edge on the butter knife. Like me, it wasn't going to be the sharpest instrument in the drawer, but it would do in a pinch. We had walked far enough that there were a few scrubby trees around. There wasn't enough to use to build a shelter, but I we could at least have a fire that night. I used the knife to cut a few smaller branches for kindling. I found a limber branch and used my shoe lace to form a bow with it. With some pocket lint and a certain feminine product from Tye's purse, I was able to get an ember glowing. With a little blowing, we had a good fire in no time.

There wasn't any material for a shelter, so we just huddled by the fire and used our bodies to share warmth. In the morning, we were fast asleep leaning against one another. It took me several minutes of stretching to get my body to obey my mind again. All it wanted to do was cramp up and complain. I didn't have time for that. We needed to get some more distance between us and the city.

About noon, which was just a guess since neither of us had a watch, we started coming into some rolling hills with more woods. I was so grateful. Rolling hills meant valleys and valleys meant the possibility of gathered water, maybe even a stream or a creek. Things were looking up. I found a small stream nearby with halfway clear water. We would have to boil the water to keep from getting sick, but that was no problem because we had the tin can I picked up and we could always start another fire.

I decided we'd camp soon. I could have gone several more miles, but Tye needed some nutrition in her and so did our son. I didn't know for sure that it was a boy, but Saul had said as much, so I was gonna assume that the baby was a he. Using the two liter bottle, I fashioned a minnow trap. If I couldn't bring down a couple of squirrels or rabbits with the crude slingshot I built using the inner tube and a forked stick, then at least we'd have minnow soup. As it turned out, I killed one of each and we had the soup as an appetizer for our fried rabbit and squirrel. It was difficult skinning them using my modified knife, but I managed to get the job done without using too much meat.

If it was just me, I could have stayed there forever. I built a lean-to shelter for us. It wasn't much, just enough space for the two of us to snuggle into for the night. I kept having to remind myself that we were only that close to share body heat, and I think Tye had to remind herself of the same thing.

Like I said, I could have stayed there for a long time. We had everything we needed. We had food and water, and with just a little ingenuity, time and some crude tools, I could build a decent shelter. But it wasn't just me, and it wasn't just Tye. We had to think about the baby and its needs. By the time we ate our dinner and had the shelter built, it was time for bed.

That night a dry thunderstorm moved through. There was no rain, just a lot of lightning and thunder, more reminders that we needed a more permanent shelter. When we said our prayers that night, we especially prayed for God to provide a sign for us to follow so that we could find the refuge we so desperately needed. Just as I dozed off, I looked up at a flash of lightning. It illuminated the night sky, and in its glow, I saw a cross over one of the hills to our north. I made note of where it was and drew a little diagram in the dirt by our bed to be sure I could find it the next day. I slept that night a sweet dreamless sleep. I didn't mind dreaming, but after forty years of it, and especially after the previous couple of weeks, I didn't need any more for a while.

The next morning, I speared a couple of small fish from the creek using a stick I had sharpened. With a little garlic, some butter and some salt, it wouldn't have been a bad breakfast. As it was, it was one of the most delicious meals I had ever had. I made a soup of sorts by boiling the fish heads and some other parts we didn't eat. It wasn't very good, but we needed all the protein and nutrition we could get.

Tye had seen the cross too and was eager to get going. We hiked with a little bit of spring in our steps. It's amazing what a little hope in a desperate situation will do to

We weren't sure what we'd find when we got there, wherever there was, but what we found wasn't disappointing in the least. It was a small cabin, probably an old hunter's shelter built years ago. It wasn't the Ritz-Carlton, but it was for us that night.

We approached cautiously, unsure that it was really abandoned. It appeared to be, but one thing I had learned over the last several weeks was that appearances can be deceiving. I made Tye hang back while I went forward for a better look. She protested, of course, but I convinced her to be safe rather than sorry. As it turned out, no one was there. I knocked anyway, just to be polite, but no one came to the door.

The door knob turned easily and I slipped inside, allowing Tye to step up onto the porch while I made sure no one was hiding under the bed. Oh, what a wonderful word. There was a real bed, with a real mattress and even some covers. Did I say it wasn't the Ritz? I was wrong. There couldn't have been a finer five star luxury resort on the planet at that moment.

Tye came in and we inspected the one room cabin even closer, looking for some more supplies. I was hoping for a better knife and maybe some canned food. We found the latter, but not the former. Oh well, you can't have everything in this life. We had just

about found all there was to find when we spotted
together the greatest treasure either of us had ever
seen. It was a copy of the Book of John, It wasn't the
entire Bible. It wasn't even a copy of the Gideon's
New Testament, but it was the best thing we could
have ever seen. We spent the rest of the remaining
daylight hours poring over the text.

We read about the Jews rejecting the Word, the
marriage at Cana, Nicodemus coming to Jesus by
night, the Samaritan woman at the well, and the pool
of Bethesda. It was so exciting to read the Word of
God. I thought of all the times when I was a kid and
Zeke and Martha would try to get me to read and
memorize the Bible. I took it for granted, thinking I
would always have it, like a reference manual I could
turn to for problems, but not as a guide for life.
Reading through that one gospel reminded me that the
God of the universe was kind enough to speak to us
one on one. He came to his own and his own received
him not. And for a long time, I received him not. It
took forty years of sleep, the death of the only people
I had ever truly loved, and a set of circumstances that
would rival any movie to get me to truly trust God,
but he did it all to bring me to him.

Before bedding down for the night, I balanced the
tin can on the door knob and brought in a bunch of
dry leaves to put under the only window. I also found
a stick to put over the window so that it would be
hard, if not impossible to open. There was no way to
lock the door and no chair to block it, so I would have

to depend on my tin can alarm to wake me in case of trouble. It worked.

The next morning, the sound of a tin can falling to the floor woke me. I was up and on the floor with my knife in hand before the can settled good on the floor.

"Whoa, brother," the big man in front of me said. He was about six foot tall, with a large build, but most of it soft fat. I registered him as not much of a threat.

"Who are you?" I demanded. Tye was up and behind me.

"I was sent to fetch you and bring you to our sanctuary," he said. "I'm Jerome. We own this cabin."

"Who are we?" I asked. I didn't real feel threatened, especially by this guy. He was as nervous as a long tailed cat in a room fool of rocking chairs, and all I had to threaten him with was a sharpened butter knife. But he looked at as if I held a bloody axe.

"We're Christians," he finally stammered. "We use this cabin to help weary travelers. We stock it with necessities, like food and bedding. But we also put the gospel of John in here as a test. If someone picks it up and reads it, then we assume that they're Christians. We've had several copies destroyed by others who aren't, but that's a small price to pay in order to find true brothers and sisters."

"How did you know?" I asked, lowering my knife and finally sheathing it in the makeshift sheath I had made from part of the inner tube. He pointed to the corner and I saw a little bit of something shine in the morning sun. He said it was a camera and that they had watched us read the book. He also assured us that the camera's lens wouldn't reach to the bed so we had a little bit of privacy. After a few more questions and some reasonable answers, he led us to the camp where the rest of the congregation gathered.

It was a small community of no more than a hundred people, if everyone showed themselves. I had the sense that there were more nearby who remained hidden. That was wise, in case we weren't who we claimed to be. When we reached the center of the compound a man with an air of authority approached us.

"Brother Blue?" he asked.

"How did you know my name?" I wondered.

"In order to survive as long as we have out here, we have to have spies in the city. We actually have a rather large network of people sympathetic to our needs. They aren't all Christians, mind you. Some are Jews who haven't yet recognized their Messiah; others are those with the new bodies who have become disillusioned with society and its lack of morality. But we have heard of you. We just didn't realize you had a companion."

"I'm sorry," I said. "This is Tye Chee. She's my fiancée. In fact, if one of you could do the honors, we'd like to get married as soon as possible. It doesn't matter who, a preacher, pastor. I'd settle for a rabbi or a justice of the peace. We just want to be married."

"I see," he said, eyeing Tye's baby bump.

"No, you don't," I said, offended that they would assume something like that, even though I knew what it looked like. I guess I couldn't blame him for assuming something like that, but it offended her honor and that offended me. "I'll be glad to explain it to whoever can marry us."

"I can do that," he said. "Come on inside our dining hall and have some lunch. Over lunch you can explain. Then afterwards the two of you can clean up and this evening we can have a wedding."

Over sandwiches and glasses of milk, I explained everything to Brother James, the man who greeted us in the compound. He was very sympathetic to our plight. That is, until he understood the origin of the baby Tye was carrying. While we were talking, he became very agitated about the baby and what it stood for, but he didn't say anything then.

Tye and I were separated after lunch. I didn't like it. I didn't ever want to be apart from her again, but we both needed baths and clean clothes and couldn't very well be together to do that. We had remained chaste so far, although the desire and temptation was almost more than I could stand at times. Even with all of the crazy circumstances of our recent lives, I felt more temptation to sleep with Tye, who remained fully clothed, than I had ever felt with a fully nude Jackee. And yet at the same time, I had greater restraint and showed Tye more respect. It was a puzzle to be sure.

When I finally saw her again, just before the wedding, I was absolutely stunned. She had always been beautiful to me, from the first moment I saw her, but now she was absolutely radiant. I know guys use a pick up line about heaven missing an angel and all that, but I could have sworn at that moment that she was truly an angel sent from God's throne just to please me, and I wouldn't have been far from being right. Maybe she wasn't truly an angel, but she was sent by God and she was sent for me to enjoy her beauty and splendor all the rest of our days.

The wedding went by like a blur. It was a condensed version of what would have happened in the days before the world went crazy, but it was still one of the greatest moments of my life. Afterwards, they allowed us the best accommodations in the compound, a large room with its own bathroom off to the side and a real queen sized feather bed. But because of the baby and the circumstances of her pregnancy, we decided to hold off on consummating our marriage vows. Man, that was a hard decision.

The next morning, instead of a group of well wishers, we were greeted by five stern faced men, including James.

"How can I help you?" I asked.

"That baby must die," he stated as if he were talking about a deformed calf or some unwanted pup.

"Over my dead body," I said, placing myself between Tye and the men. I reached for the knife I still kept in its homemade sheath at the small of my back.

"That baby is the seed of the devil," he proclaimed. "It is God's will that it die."

"You take one more step and you'll be able to ask God yourself," I stated calmly and I meant every word. People like this made me sick. It was people who just knew they were doing God's will that took me from the only parents I ever knew. And that just because we didn't have the same skin color. For people who believed in the brotherhood of Christianity, we sure did behave like a dysfunctional family sometimes.

I watched James the most, but my peripheral vision was also keeping tabs on the two to his immediate left and right. The other two hung back altogether. I figured they were only there because they had been drafted for numbers sake. They probably figured that I would back down from five men. They figured wrong. First of all, I knew that I wasn't facing five men. I was only really facing one man, the leader.

The two in the back would bolt at the first sign of blood, and there was fixing to be plenty of it if they didn't back away from my child.

The other two were inching forward slowly, like molasses on a chilly day. I wasn't going to give them the chance to get any closer. I stepped forward quickly, pulling the knife from my sheath as I did. Before they had a chance to respond, I had it pressed hard into James' gut, cutting his shirt slightly. Oh well, send me the dry cleaning bill later. I'll also pay for the pants you just soiled.

"Take one more step and you'll see what James had for breakfast this morning," I warned. They inched a little closer and I pressed a little harder.

"Back off," James demanded.

"The only abortion happening today is gonna be me aborting your intestines." I proclaimed.

"Enough," a voice stated. I wasn't going to turn and see where it came from. "I said enough." An old man came from behind the other men, who parted for him like the Red Sea. He looked to be at least a hundred years old, maybe two.

"My name is Brother Andrew," he said. "Would you please remove your weapon from Brother James' stomach? We don't need bloodshed here today."

"I'm not moving anything as long as my child is

threatened." I said flatly. This seemed to shock the old man.

"Brother James, I should let him gut you like the lifeless fish you are. We discussed this in the council meeting last night. We are not in the place of God to take a life, even if we suspect that child to be the Anti-Christ." Okay, so someone had finally said it. I thought it all along. I suspected that my child, the one I would help raise and call my own, the one who would make little stick drawings of himself me and his mama would one day be a vessel for Satan's takeover of the world, but I still wouldn't allow anyone to kill him now. Because now he was just an innocent child, like any other child. It would be up to God whether or not he became the incarnation of evil, and who knows, maybe with the right upbringing and lots and lots of prayers, he may be the one who stands against Satan in the end and leads countless souls to Jesus. I wasn't holding my breath, but I knew God was capable of anything.

"So no one is threatening Tye or our baby?" I asked. This whole time, Tye had been quietly praying. She was the real warrior in the room.

"No one," Brother Andrew assured me, "but we will have to ask you to leave. We'll provide transportation and supplies for your journey, but we cannot risk the whole compound for the sake of one child."

"Even though one child gave his life for you?" I

asked. It was a low blow, I know, but I wasn't feeling the most charming at that moment.

"I'm afraid our faith is not what it should be," he confessed. "I'm afraid it will face greater testing than this soon. Will you accept our offer?"

"Where should we go?" I asked, releasing the pressure on Brother James' stomach ever so slightly. I still felt like doing some exploratory surgery.

"There is a community of believers to the west. They call themselves New Egypt. It's because so many saint went to Egypt for sanctuary at times."

"We'll accept," I said, getting a nod from Tye. She was amazing.

I withdrew my knife from Brother James and he almost collapsed. That was the difference between men like him and me. He could only handle confrontation when it was easy and in his favor. Me? I had been raised in confrontation. It was basically all I knew from the age of three or four. Looking back, I treasured all of those moments, every fight, every bloody nose or chipped tooth because looking ahead at my life, I had the feeling I would need every bit of wisdom gained from those moments.

Brother Andrew led us to a three wheeled vehicle at the west of the compound. It had two wheels in the front and a single wheel in the rear, but it wasn't like any motorcycle or tricycle I had ever seen. I had waited for some kind of technology to impress me in this century and here it was. Instead of the usual seating that a normal vehicle of that type might have, it had an open cockpit body with two seats and just a little cargo space behind the seats. The controls looked like something out of a sci-fi movie. He showed me how it worked and we test drove it around the compound before he gave me the final instructions on how to get to New Egypt.

Before we left, Brother Andrew gave me his old 45 caliber service revolver from that he had gotten from his years as a police officer. I argued against taking such a weapon, one that had a personal attachment, but he insisted.

"I should have gotten rid of it long ago," he said."It's a reminder of another day and another man."

After a quick lunch, Tye and I rode off to the west, in the direction of New Egypt. One lone cowboy, his beautiful bride and very possibly their Anti-Christ baby riding off into the sunset.

So let me summarize this, for my sake more than anyone else's. I'm a modern day Rip Van Winkle, awakened to a world where wrong is right and right is wrong, riding off to New Egypt with my virgin bride who happens to be three months pregnant with a hybrid child of nanobots and human flesh, who may or may not be the Anti-Christ. I'm sure glad nothing weird ever happens to me.

I know one thing. We're not calling him Damien.

EPILOGUE

This part of the story was related to me by Julius Erving. No, not the basketball player, the Jew who helped keep the books for the maniac known as Saul. Sometime after this event, he escaped from Saul and made his way to New Egypt, but only after stopping at a certain cabin and reading the Book of John. He wasn't a Christian when he went in the cabin, but he was when he came out. Anyway, this is what he said happened after our escape.

"The transponders have failed, sir," a military man reported to Saul. "We have no way of tracking them."

"No matter," Saul said nonchalantly. "We know they are headed to New Egypt."

"Should we send out some troops to intervene," the military commander asked. "We could intercept them before they arrive."

"No," Saul said forcefully. "This is that which is written, 'I must call my son out of Egypt'."